ANSWER MAN

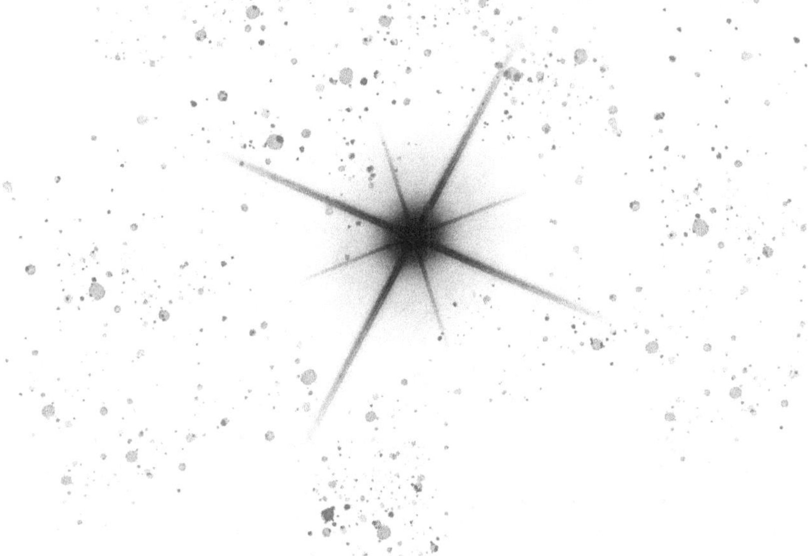

by MARK DONAHUE

D!

DONAHUE
LITERARY PROPERTIES

ACKNOWLEDGEMENT

IN 2018, MY WIFE MARSHA and I went to Aliencon in Pasadena. I, at least, expected weird. After all, the premise is based on a TV show that purports that Earth was visited by aliens thousands of years ago. That those visits helped shape our civilization, our cultures, and to a great extent our present day lives. After 4 days, it didn't seem all that weird. Neither did the PhD's, scientists, and military personnel whom we met. They were serious.

This book acknowledges that we don't know all that much about what's "out there." But I applaud those who dare to look up and ask questions. Who challenge norms. Even risk criticism. To those who ask difficult questions and are not afraid of the answers.

Dedicated to:
Those who man the telescopes.
Who know we are not alone, and never were.

PROLOGUE

LIFELESS AND FRIGID, A SLATE gray rock, the size of a major Midwestern city, sped through the darkness somewhere between Jupiter and Mars as it had done for billions of years. Its speed averaged over 62,000 miles per hour, varying based on the gravitational pull exerted on it from the millions of objects it passed on its journey through the void.

Its area was nearly twenty square miles shaped like an imperfect rectangle. Made up of a mixture of elements including oxygen, silicon, iron, nickel, and magnesium, its precise weight was incalculable, but its precise potential for devastation was immeasurable.

It was one of millions in the asteroid belt, but unlike some, it didn't rotate around its principle axis but rather tumbled chaotically through the void like a knuckleball thrown on a windless day in Yankee Stadium.

The rock was well-known to the two astronomers who had been following its progress, or more importantly, its revised path and ultimate destination.

"Why the change?"

"Has to be Jupiter."

"Yeah, has to be Jupiter."

"What do you think?"

"The numbers don't lie."

"I know the damn numbers don't lie, but what do you think?"

"I think we're fucked."

"Yeah, I think we're pretty much fucked too."

CHAPTER 1

ON THE CAMPUS OF MIT in Cambridge, Massachusetts, hundreds of fashion-challenged but intellectually blessed students, many with their noses buried in a book, moved to their next class on an unusually cool early summer day.

One student was stopped by a nondescript old man and handed an envelope. The student took, then looked at the envelope and nodded. The old man nodded and walked away without speaking.

The student, a graduate assistant, entered the Kavli Institute for Astrophysics and Space Research and walked down a nearly deserted marble hallway for several yards. He stopped at an office with the name of Dr. Mei Liu, PhD, on a placard. He knocked on the mahogany-and-glass door, but there was no answer. He opened the door with his key and saw that the room was empty. He tossed the envelope on Dr. Liu's desk and left the office.

CHAPTER 2

AT THE AL JAZEERA NETWORK station in Doha, Qatar, Iranian-born, Harvard-educated, acerbic TV host Abir Ahmad was having his final makeup applied in his dressing room in preparation for his nightly worldwide broadcast that focused on the Middle East. A young page entered the dressing room and handed him an envelope.

"What the hell is this crap?" Abir asked, living up to his reputation.

"I don't know, Mr. Ahmad. An old man walked up and gave it to me on my way back from lunch. He told me to give it to you right away."

"Who was this man?"

"I don't know, sir; I never saw him before."

"What did he look like?"

"He looked old, sir."

CHAPTER 3

AT THE VATICAN RESIDENCE IN Rome, Father José Peña, a youthful-looking forty-four-year-old priest who had been raised in Cuba, was laying on his bed in his underwear and a Miami Dolphins sweatshirt. He sucked on a cherry Tootsie Roll Pop and listened to the Doobie Brothers on an antiquated tape player, as he scanned the latest *Sports Illustrated* swimsuit edition. There was an annoying and persistent knock on his door.

After the third knock, he said, "No one here," hoping whoever it was would believe him and finally go away.

They didn't believe him, but they did go away after sliding an envelope under his door.

After staring at the envelope for several minutes and waiting for "China Grove" to end, Father Peña grudgingly rose from his bed and opened the envelope, took out the letter, and read it. As he did, a smile crossed his face. "Hope the hell this works."

CHAPTER 4

AT YANKEE STADIUM, FORMER U.S. president Robert Mitchell was sitting with his wife, some friends, and two large Secret Service agents behind home plate. They ate ice cream from plastic baseball helmets and nibbled on salted peanuts still in the shells. They watched the Yankees get their asses kicked by Toronto.

From behind them an envelope was passed person-to-person down several rows of bleacher seats before finally being handed to Mitchell by a ten-year-old boy wearing a faded A-Rod T-shirt. Mitchell opened the envelope and read the letter inside. He turned and asked the boy, "Who gave you this envelope?"

The boy shrugged and said, "I don't know, it came from back up there," pointing behind him.

CHAPTER 5

AT THE SETI INSTITUTE IN Mountain View, California, a young, handsome, long-haired astronomer, Dr. William (Billy) Gregorie, was hitting on an attractive young woman over a brown bag lunch in his office.

"C'mon, honey, the doors are locked, and I won't say a word to anybody. It'll be between just you and me."

"Are you kidding me? I didn't get my master's in astronomy just to get laid under an intergalactic antenna," the blue-eyed, raven-haired stargazer said.

"Ever tried it? I mean this could be an awe-inspiring, life-changing event on many levels."

"No, and I'm particularly not going to try it with you. By the way, where's your girlfriend, the one from Berkeley, the blonde?"

"Can you imagine? She had the temerity to dump me."

"Wow, there's a shocker. Ever consider a change in your relationship strategy, you know, to maybe include monogamy as a building block?"

"No, actually, I never did think of such a restrictive and antiquated rule as being part of a relationship. And now that I do think about it, it sounds boring. You mean today's young women deem such a horrific concept as important?"

"You know, all the girls were right, you are kind of a pig. A really smart pig, but a pig."

"The chance of a lifetime and you, what's the word, demurred?"

"No, actually, I just told you to go fuck *yourself*, doctor."

"I was afraid that was what you said," Billy said, a sincere sadness in his voice.

Without knocking, an older woman entered the room from the door that was not so locked, much to the surprise of the younger woman. The older woman walked to the table where Billy and his assistant were seated. She handed Billy an envelope. "Thanks. What's this, a paternity suit?" he asked, hoping it wasn't a paternity suit.

"I don't what it is, but it was marked urgent and so I thought I'd interrupt your star listening for a moment and bring it in. Surprised the door wasn't locked."

"Why would I ever need to lock my door?" Billy asked innocently.

The older woman pointed to Billy and addressed the younger woman. "Careful with that one, he's trouble," she said on her way out of the room.

Billy opened the envelope and read the letter inside. He appeared perplexed. With no explanation or further conversation, he left his office, and a somewhat confused young woman who was very grateful she had "demurred."

CHAPTER 6

ON A WARM SUNDAY MORNING at the Lord Is My Shepherd Baptist Church in Cairo, Alabama, Reverend John B. Johnson was on a roll. He had already been preaching at full volume to his all-black congregation for over an hour, and he was just getting warmed up. So was his audience, willing to take on that damn devil himself right then and there if Reverend John gives them the word.

Sweating profusely through his white shirt and gray suit and wiping his face with a red bath towel, Reverend John didn't let up a bit. "Brothers and sisters, the Lord sees everything ya do. Ain't no hidin'. No use shuttin' the doors or turnin' off the lights. The Man sees it all! Sees it all!!"

In the middle of Reverend John's stirring sermon about life in heaven and salvation of the soul, an eighty-eight-year-old black woman named Elsie, who hadn't been to church since 1953, walked slowly up the aisle and handed him an envelope. As the church grew quiet, Reverend John took the envelope and nodded to the old woman, who nodded back. She turned and walked slowly out of the church without uttering a word.

Reverend John opened the envelope in front of his congregation and looked at the contents. He raised his arms in victory and shouted to his audience, "Hallelujah, hallelujah, praise the Lord!"

CHAPTER 7

AT THE BEVERLY WILSHIRE HOTEL patio restaurant in Los Angles, Stephan Connor sipped peach iced tea. At thirty-six-years-old, he had only recently retired after selling his social media site for three billion dollars. He thought he should have gotten four.

Stephan was tall, skinny, good-looking, arrogant, and bored. He was sitting alone, wearing baggy blue jeans and an Eagles T-shirt. Looking out through his blue-framed Ray-Ban Wayfarers from under the brim of his LA Dodgers hat, he looked longingly at the seemingly endless number of beautiful women who glided by, just out of his reach in many ways. He concluded he would miss them a great deal.

An old man walked to the railing next to his table and handed Stephan an envelope, then walked away without acknowledging him. Stephan read the letter inside, immediately checked his watch, stepped over the railing, and walked slowly down Wilshire Boulevard.

He was no longer bored.

CHAPTER 8

IN A SECLUDED WOODED AREA four miles outside Aspen, Colorado, a high-pitched, almost imperceptible whirring sound was heard, similar to a gyroscope being pulled by a string.

Moments later, a forty-something, handsome, well-built, dark-haired man named David, walked out of the treeline and headed toward a 10,000 square foot home perched on the side of a long undulating ski run. He carried a Mont Blanc briefcase, wore running shorts, a Polo tennis shirt, Tom Ford Limited Collection sunglasses, and Nike cross training shoes with no socks.

After a short walk through a wooded area with a crushed-stone pathway, the air thick with the aroma of pine and chokecherry, he entered through the unlocked back door of the large house and tossed his suitcase in the corner of an ecru-colored leather sectional couch. He moved quickly to the kitchen, opened the fridge, grabbed a beer and a bag of corn chips, flopped down in an overstuffed chair, and put his feet on the ottoman. "Damn, what a day," he said to no one, since he was alone in the house.

After a few sips of his beer and a handful of chips, he flipped on ESPN and caught the latest baseball scores from the games back East already underway. After getting that vital information, he turned and gazed through the huge picture window at the beautiful valley that stretched for miles into the distance like a verdant tunnel lined with a dozen shades of green. A few moments later his cell rang, and he answered on speaker.

"Just got here a few minutes ago" he said.

"Any problems?" a male voice asked.

"Nope."

"What about the letters?"

"I have confirmation they all got the letters last week."

"What do you think?" the male voice asked.

"I don't know. But the deadline to respond is tomorrow at midnight. It was a good offer. I bet they'll all show."

"It's important they do, or we have to move on."

"What's the rush?" David asked between sips of Budweiser.

"Our people are getting impatient. I'm getting impatient. C'mon, you know this is important."

"I know it's important, but what else can we do? Either they take the offer, or they don't. You know how this goes." David said as he watched Red Sox–Tampa Bay highlights from Fenway Park.

"Get some rest, you old buzzard. You're not as young as you used to be, ya know."

"Go fuck yourself. Talk to you in two days. Bye."

After David hung up, he tossed the cell on the couch, and walked outside to the huge deck that encircled the rear of the glass-and red-brown, three-level, cedar house. He looked at the spectacular view and breathed in the early summer mountain air. He shut his eyes; for nearly ten minutes he basked in the warm late afternoon sun as if in a meditative trance.

Later that night David sat on the sectional, drank beer, and ate warmed-up pizza while he watched a baseball game. Between the third and fourth innings he looked over a copy of the letter that had been delivered to the seven people who had made his final list. People who he hoped would soon be his house guests, and eventually with appropriate encouragement, his working partners.

Hello,

My name is David.

You have been chosen to receive this letter and its content, so that you can help Earth survive a pending natural disaster. Your selection to attend a meeting to discuss this critical situation was based on factors that will be abundantly clear to you when we convene.

To encourage your attendance, please find enclosed a cashier's check for $100,000 to cover your travel expenses and time. Please cash this check prior to your departure to ensure its legitimacy. For those not requiring financial assistance, please feel free to donate your check to a favorite charity.

I realize this request is unusual, and you have many questions. But I urge you to accept this invitation in the good faith that it was intended. Please arrive promptly at the location described below. To refuse is to put at risk the ongoing survival of Earth and the life inhabiting it.

Please travel alone.

To ensure this letter is not passed to others, the paper on which it is written will self-destruct five minutes after the letter is touched by you. Therefore, it would be unwise to put it and the check in a pocket.

Your friend,

David.

After rereading the invitation for about the tenth time, David said to himself, "They'll be here." Several minutes later he fell asleep and missed the last three innings of a Dodgers beatdown of the Giants behind a two-hitter by Clayton Kershaw.

CHAPTER 9

EARLY THE NEXT MORNING, A sleek Gulfstream G-650 made a smooth landing at the Aspen Airport and taxied to a stop in front of a hangar. The pilot was Stephan Connor, who wore a blue work shirt, old jeans, and a wrinkled suede sport coat. He hesitated at the door of the jet to gather himself before he walked down the stairs. He was met by two of the local ground crew. "Not sure how long I'll be here, so keep it inside, and I'll text you guys when I know my plans."

The two men nodded, shook Stephan's hand, and began to hook up the $65 million jet to the natural gas--powered "tug" that would move it to the private hangar that Stephan had reserved the day before.

Stephan carried a small gym bag over his shoulder and walked to a waiting Range Rover, entered the SUV, and drove off by himself.

At the same time, the other recipients of David's letters were in various modes of travel, including airplanes, trains, buses, and cars, as they made their way to Aspen. All traveled alone.

Less than thirty minutes after arriving at the Aspen Airport, Stephan pulled up in front of David's house. He exited and checked the address on the mailbox before making his way to the front door. He rang the doorbell twice, but there was no answer.

Stephan walked around the entire outside of the house, which appeared deserted, and returned to where he had started and peered through the glass front door but saw no one. He tried the door, and to his surprise, it opened. He entered. "Hello, anybody home? Hello? Is there a David here? Hello?"

When Stephan walked into the family room, a sleepy looking man with mussed dark hair slowly arose from the sectional couch. He wore earphones and when he looked back at Stephan, he accidently knocked over his bottle of beer from the night before onto the coffee table. The tepid lager trickled down to the floor creating a small puddle.

"Fuck me. Hey, Stephan, grab me a towel from the kitchen, will you?" David asked.

Stephan looked around the huge country kitchen with copper pots and pans suspended on hooks above the stove and yanked several paper towels from the holder next to the double sink.

"Here you go," he said as he handed the paper towels to David.

David got down on his hands and knees and sopped up the beer from the table and floor. "Christ, you're kind of early, aren't you?"

"Left Burbank around 5 a.m. Sounded like you wanted me to be on time, so here I am."

"Come in on the 650?"

"Yeah."

"Nice ride. Fly it yourself?"

"Yeah, like always."

"That's kind of risky, isn't it?"

"I was a pilot in the military; I know what I'm doing," Stephan said.

"I know you know what you're doing."

"Seems like you know a lot about me."

"That's right, I do." David said.

"Then you know I'm always early. You know, like the bird."

"That's okay. Bet the rest of the folks won't be here for hours. You hungry?" David asked.

"I could eat. But I'd rather know what the fuck this is all about," Stephan said.

"Omelet, okay?"

"Sure."

"Ham, cheese, mushroom, and tomato?" David asked.

"Sounds good."

David started banging around the kitchen in his Jockey underwear and T-shirt. He beat up six eggs, chopped ham and mushrooms, made hash browns, and dropped rye bread into the toaster, right before he placed fresh grated Swiss cheese on top of his masterpiece. As David cooked, Stephan made the coffee, poured orange juice, and brought out the ketchup, coffee creamer, and hot sauce.

After the men sat down and began to attack their omelets, David asked, "Who'd you give the hundred grand to?"

"A no-kill shelter I support back in LA."

"Good move."

"You realize I have a lot of questions, right?" Stephan asked.

"Figured you would."

After several moments of silence, Stephan asked, "Fair to say you're gonna wait until the others get here before telling me what's going on?"

"Fair to say. Easier to tell everyone all at once. Want jelly for your toast?"

"Got strawberry?"

After he checked the pantry, David said, "Here it is....all the comforts..."

"Speaking of home, where'd you come in from, David"?

"Florida. Miami."

"How long did that take?"

"About fifteen minutes," David said.

Stephan laughed.

CHAPTER 10

AFTER BREAKFAST, STEPHAN AND DAVID lay in the sun on the deck and sipped iced tea as they waited for the others.

"How long have you lived in Miami?"

"About twenty years."

"Where'd you go to school?"

"No place you've heard of," David said.

"Married?"

"No."

"You work?" Stephan asked.

"Guess you could say I'm a developer."

"Aren't we all?"

After several more minutes of silence, Stephan said, "Real talkative bastard, aren't you?"

"I've been told I have my moments."

"Can't wait."

"I'll bet you'll find the wait worthwhile," David said

After he tried and failed several more times to get David to open up and spill the beans about the upcoming meeting, Stephan finally gave up. Instead, the men spent most of the afternoon talking about books, movies, and baseball, including a rather spirited baseball trivia contest that David won.

Later in the afternoon, David hit the shower and asked Stephan to get the door if any of the other guests showed up. Within fifteen minutes the front doorbell rang. Stephan opened the door and said hello to the unlikely duo of Abir Ahmad, originally from somewhere near Cairo, Egypt, and John Johnson from suburban Cairo, Alabama.

Opening the door with a smile, Stephan said, "Gentlemen, welcome to Aspen. Please come in."

"I ain't comin' in nowhere till you tell me who the hell you are and what's this all about," John Johnson announced.

"I'd gladly tell you what this is all about, but I'm not your host, and so far he isn't talking. But come on in. It's safe and the beer's cold," Stephan said.

The men entered the house, although John Johnson did so with obvious trepidation. After some small talk, Abir looked at Stephan and asked, "You look familiar. Do I know you?"

"I'm Stephan Connor, founder of Open Book. I was a guest on your show; you interviewed me a few years ago after the sale of my company."

"I indeed remember you. I thought you should have gotten four billion."

"You're right, I should have."

"Do you have any idea what the hell we're doing here?" Abir asked.

"Not sure. I got the same letter you did, so I came to see what's up," Stephan said.

"How many invited to this little party?" Abir asked.

"David said there were seven of us."

After walking around and gaping at the inside of the beautiful home, John asked. "Who the hell exactly is this David guy?"

"All I know is he seems like a good guy and he's our host. He's in the shower now. Should be out in a few minutes. Who wants a beer?" Stephan asked.

The men moved to the kitchen, opened beers, and found a bag of pretzels.

"I'll tell you what, this is damn strange. I 'spect you all got the hundred grand?" John asked.

The other two men nodded.

"Lotta green for a damn meetin'."

John was interrupted by the doorbell. Stephan opened the door and greeted Dr. William (Billy) Gregorie, SETI researcher; Dr. Mei Liu, physicist from MIT, and former president Robert Mitchell, who wore a Yankees cap and sunglasses.

"Hello folks, welcome to the party. Guess we're missing just one now," Stephan said.

Stephan recognized the former president when he removed his hat and glasses. "Mr. President? I must say the guest list has just taken a quantum leap in exclusivity."

"Hello, Stephan. What a nice thing to say given that you donated several million dollars to see I wasn't reelected."

"What happened to the sanctity of secrecy in political donations?"

"Down the toilet, like everything else in D.C."

"Where are your Secret Service groupies?"

"After seven years, I can lose those guys when I want to. And after reading David's letter, I wanted to."

Over the next thirty minutes, the group of six stood in the kitchen, drank beer, laughed, and talked. David finally emerged from the bathroom, drying his hair with a towel. He wore baggy running shorts, a white tennis shirt, and flip-flops. He held a cell phone to his ear and nonchalantly waved and smiled to the group as he walked past them, while he opened a cold beer.

"No problem, Father. Where are you now? O'Hare or Midway? Okay then, tell you what, grab a cab and make it to the front gate at Soldier Field and meet me on the Lake Shore Drive side. I'll be there in an hour with some friends I think you'll enjoy meeting. See you soon."

The other six were intrigued at the sight of David, a guy who had ponied up $700,000 for a little party, but they were stunned by what they had just heard.

"Excuse me, but did you just say you were going to meet someone in Chicago in an hour?" Robert asked.

"I didn't want to have to rush," David said with a smile.

"Is this some kind of *Punk'd* TV show or what? What the fuck is going on? And who the hell are you?" Billy asked.

"Folks, I am truly very sorry. I lay down for a few minutes just to rest, fell asleep, and was very rude not to be here to greet each of you as you arrived. Let's start over. My name is David, and I'm your host here in beautiful Aspen for a few days. I trust everyone had a good trip?"

Let's get something straight," Billy said. "I cashed your check and put the money in a safe spot, so I felt I should at least be polite and show up. But if I don't get some answers, I'm heading back to California right now."

"That's certainly your privilege, Dr. Gregorie. In fact, if you like, we can drop you off on our way to Chicago. But please stay just a few minutes and let me explain some things. You see, that's why I've asked all of you here—to explain some things. Some things you very much need to know, and some other things you may have always wanted to know. Please, it's more comfortable in the family room."

David led the way, and the group silently filed into the family room and sat on the large sectional couch. The setting sun shone in the group's faces and they squinted slightly as David stood in front of the window and began to talk. His face was partially hidden in shadow.

"You were all invited here because each of you talk to and speak for millions of people around the world. Or you possess a special knowledge or expertise. You are all successful, intelligent, and from what I can surmise, open-minded, despite what you may say on TV, in the pulpit, in front of peers, or to world leaders. Those are important traits for my needs, and for the needs of Earth."

"What the hell are you talking about?" Billy asked.

"I'm sorry, allow me to be more direct. In less than a year, Earth will be hit by an asteroid that's over twenty miles in diameter. The impact site will be just west of Portland, Oregon. The initial impact will create an ash cloud that will kill every living thing in a teardrop pattern that will include an area east to Minneapolis and south to Texas in less than six minutes. The impact will also cause the volcanos at Mount St. Helens and under Jackson Hole, Wyoming, to erupt simultaneously. Those explosions will incinerate what's left of the world in a fireball that will circle the globe in mere hours."

The group of six looked at David in stunned silence. As they did, the sun sank deeper into the horizon, causing the colors on their faces to become considerably darker.

"You paid each of us a $100,000 and brought us from all over the world to listen to this nonsense?" Abir said sarcastically.

"Mr. Ahmad—may I call you Abir? I think there may be one among you who might offer a respected form of confirmation as to what I'm saying."

The group was silent and looked nervously at each other. Mei Liu, a beautiful, Beijing-born, Princeton-educated PhD and MIT professor, spoke in a hushed tone.

"How did you know?" she asked. "We just confirmed it last week. And how can you be so sure of its new path at this point?"

"We have been tracking Big Ben for several hundred years now and knew that because of Jupiter's gravity, you may have originally and erroneously calculated it was going to miss the Earth. Right, Mei?"

"That is true, but our most recent data, received by us only two weeks ago and confirmed by astrophysicists and observatories all over the world, has indicated that there will be a direct hit in the area you mentioned."

"Oh my God," Robert said. "David, how did you know such a thing?"

"We're pretty good at math," David said.

"What do you mean, you've been 'tracking this thing for several hundred years,'" Billy asked. "Is this some kind of joke?"

"Believe me, an asteroid that size, at that speed hitting Earth, is not a joke, unless you consider the end of life on this planet a joke," David said.

"Mei, you mean he's right about that big rock and the damage it will cause?" Abir asked.

"Yes, unfortunately, he's right," Mei said.

"David, you keep saying 'we.' Who's 'we'?" Stephan asked.

"Look, I could tell you guys a bunch of stuff that you won't believe and you'll just leave here thinking I'm a head case, and that's no good for you, me, or the planet. Why don't I just show you?" David suggested.

"Show us what?" Stephan asked.

"Shall we take a little ride?" David suggested with a small smile.

CHAPTER 11

DAVID LED THE PARADE TO the back door, opened it, and walked toward a wooded area as the rest of group lagged behind. Stephan jogged ahead and caught up to David.

"So, you weren't kidding about a fifteen-minute ride from Miami?"

"It was actually ten minutes, but I didn't want to brag," David said, smiling.

"Are we really going to Chicago?" Stephan asked, like a twelve-year-old asking about going to an amusement park.

"We can stop in Paris on the way if you like."

"Holy shit, this is fucking incredible," Stephan said.

The group came to a circular grass clearing in the woods about twenty-five yards in diameter. There was nothing blocking their view across the lea.

"We waiting here for a chopper?" Billy asked.

"This might be a bit faster, quieter, safer, and significantly more comfortable," David said.

David took what looked like a garage door opener from his pocket and clicked it once. Within seconds, a cigar-shaped machine suddenly appeared and hovered silently twenty feet off the ground. It was dark blue in color.

"Oh my God!" Abir said, no longer sarcastic.

The rest of the group backed away from what had suddenly appeared above them, except for Mei. She moved directly under the craft that was emitting a slight whirring sound as it levitated.

"Ion engines?" Mei asked.

"We passed that technology centuries ago. It's really just an anti-gravity, electro-magnetic device, the size of a loaf of bread, with a kind of supercharger on it. I'll explain more once we're airborne. By the way, do you like the color?"

"Yeah, very cool, I really like it." Mei said with awe in her voice.

"Is this real? And are you what I think you are?" Robert, the former president, asked.

"What do you think I am?"

"I don't really give damn as long as you're not a Republican," Robert said.

"I'm not really into politics, so you're safe," David replied.

"Where are you from?" Mei asked.

"My parents were born about five light-years from here. I was born in a ship quite a bit bigger than this one, in 1873, your time."

The rest of the group stood in silent shock as David casually spoke about things his audience found to be a mixture of the unbelievable and the preposterous.

"Folks, we'll have plenty of time for your questions, but we need get a move on. I don't want to keep Father Peña waiting. By the way, he likes to be called José," David said.

David moved the device in his hand, and the levitating craft lowered to the ground and silently widened at one end, taking on a more streamlined look. It also took on a purplish hue. A door with no apparent seams opened, and a teal colored glow emerged from inside the craft.

"Lady and gentlemen, your chariot awaits."

"I don't like flyin'. That's why I took a train out here," John Johnson said.

"I can assure I am a very good pilot, and this craft is far safer than the train you took."

John nodded but did not look convinced.

After several more moments, and led by Billy, the group walked up a six-foot ramp and entered the craft one by one. The ship measured thirty-two feet in length, fifteen feet wide, and eight feet high. The inside was of clear span construction, with tinted windows that passengers could see out of but could not be seen through from the outside.

"Prefer to sit, lie down, or stand?" David asked of his guests. His passengers looked at one another unsure how to answer.

"Here are your options," David waved the device and a chair-like object rose from the floor. Another wave, and a lounge-like object appeared. "The other option is to come up front and get a pretty good view."

As one, the group moved forward with Stephan leading way. But he suddenly stopped in his tracks. "Whoa."

The front of the craft was all glass—floor, ceiling and walls. There were no controls.

"Who the hell flies this thing?" Stephan asked.

"It's all in here," David said, then raised the handheld device.

"It's sort of like a real cool nav system with an autopilot." David explained.

"When I was president, I read secret reports of UFOs and alien craft but never got confirmation."

"We met with some of your predecessors, but they said any formal announcement about us being here would cause a panic. So we kept quiet."

"Wait a minute, you actually met with other presidents? Why wasn't I...?"

"Excuse me, Mr. President, I need to get us on our way."

David moved to a position at the front of the ship and hit a button on the device. A green-colored three-dimensional image appeared and hovered in the air. It showed a map of the United States and displayed a small pulsating light that appeared near Chicago. David touched another button and the ship rose.

"We'll be in Chicago in sixteen minutes," David said.

"Chicago's a thousand miles away," Billy said.

"A little over 900," David corrected.

"Christ, that's over four thousand..."

"We'll be traveling over six thousand miles an hour after we reach an altitude of seventy thousand feet."

"What about radar, why can't our radar see you?" Billy asked.

"C'mon, doctor. You guys have had stealth technology for decades. By the way, folks, the best sensation is to stand directly over the floor and look straight down."

The group of six did as David suggested. The craft rose slowly at first, then the ground fell away at a rate so fast that all six gasped in unison and held on to each other. Within seconds, the lights of Denver appeared as the distant yellow spots they were. The craft hung silently suspended in the air at seventy-thousand feet.

"Oh my God, this is spectacular," Mei said.

"Pretty cool, isn't it?" David agreed.

"What's holding us up here?" Billy asked.

"Really good duct tape," David said, deadpan.

The group laughed and continued to stare out the glass windows and could see darkness to the east and sunlight to the west.

"I hate to break the spell here, but what does all this have to do with the asteroid?" Mei asked.

"Tell you what, Doctor, you guys just enjoy the ride to Chicago, and we can talk over dinner after we pick up Father Peña. I made reservations for us at a place I like in Santa Barbara. Got us a private room. That okay with everyone?"

The group nodded somewhat numbly, food the last thing on their minds. David pushed another button and the craft silently accelerated into a clear Colorado night that within seconds became a clear Kansas night. They left Kansas behind and within seconds reached a cruising speed of just under seven thousand miles per hour.

"I can't hear an engine," Mei said.

"In essence, we're in a ball of antigravity matter that eliminates friction. At low altitudes like this we use a hydrogen intake engine with a form of ionization that you asked about before. If we went to deep space, things get real interesting speed-wise when we use nuclear power, but I'd need a little time with you to show you how it all comes together."

"How fast can this thing go?" Billy asked.

"How fast would you like to go?" David asked.

"Holy shit," Billy gasped.

Within twelve minutes, the lights of Chicago came into view.

CHAPTER 12

"YOU'RE NOT GOING TO LAND this thing on Michigan Avenue, are you? We might upset the locals," Billy said.

"No. But we can cruise the Magnificent Mile if you like."

The craft came over Lake Michigan with a whisper eight feet off the water. As it crossed over land, it turned right off Madison Street onto Michigan Avenue and floated silently northward.

"People can't see us?" Mei asked.

"Hell, if they did, they'd probably start shooting," David said.

"You're probably right; this is Chicago," Robert added.

The craft passed the Aon Center on its right, crossed Wacker Drive, and over the Chicago River. It moved at a steady pace thirty feet above street level toward Oak Street, then to Lake Shore Drive before turning and heading south. In the distance, Soldier Field loomed. The craft rose over the stadium's wall and landed on the twenty-five yard line.

"You guys stay here. I'll grab Father Peña, I mean José, and we'll go get some chow." David said.

David lowered the door of the craft and went to retrieve José. Still recovering from what they had heard and experienced over the previous hour, the group stared at each other in silent disbelief. Collectively, they were suffering from serious stimuli overload. What they had already seen and heard would change them, and the rest of world, forever. Things would not and could not ever be the same. That realization had an almost numbing effect.

Finally, Abir asked quietly, "Is this all a dream?"

"If it is, we're all living it together," Stephan whispered.

"We were just abducted by some damn alien, right?" John asked.

"This was an invitation to dinner, not an abduction. I think we're all here because of the asteroid he talked about," Mei said.

"Is that thing real? Is it really going to hit Earth?" Stephan asked.

"Yes, and David's explanation of the damage is accurate as well. We just confirmed it last week."

"Can't we do anything to stop it?"

"Stephan, it's so large, that even if we could blow it up, which we can't, thousands of fragments would hit the Earth and the results would be the same," Mei explained.

"David said we were invited because of the people we have access to on Earth. How's that tied to the asteroid?" Robert asked.

"Not sure, but it's clear we are all here for a reason. It's also pretty clear that dinner should be rather interesting," Mei said.

A few minutes later, David reappeared at the craft with a winded Father José Peña in tow. The men entered the craft, and David introduced everyone to the smiling priest. "Wow, this is weird. I couldn't see this ship until I was within two feet. Pretty neat."

"Seafood sound good, José?"

"Is that a gross Catholic generalization or is it Friday?"

"I'll take that as a yes," David said with a smile.

CHAPTER 13

THE CRAFT ROSE DIRECTLY OVER Chicago, but then the lighted urban landscape below began to blur and within twenty minutes the craft hovered over the Pacific Ocean facing the Biltmore Hotel in Montecito, California, with the sun still shining brightly. The craft passed over the hotel and moved a mile north toward a wooded area with a clearing visible among tall pines. They landed in silence.

"What could I get on a trade for my G-6 for this baby?" Stephan asked.

"This thing is over a hundred years old, so you might get some cash back for your G-6. Our new models would really knock your socks off."

"Holy Christ."

"Folks, just wait outside a minute. I arranged to have a vehicle waiting for us."

After the group exited the craft, it rose twenty feet into air and disappeared. David jogged to a nearby van and drove it back to the seven people who remained spellbound. After they climbed into the vehicle, David drove them to the nearby San Ysidro Ranch, where a private dining room had been set up adjacent to the Stone House Restaurant.

The setting sun, combined with the fragrances of jasmine, lavender, and a myriad of other aromatic intoxications, plus the twenty-minute trip from Chicago, had rendered the group silent. The collective thought was that if all this was a dream, it was a pretty good dream, and they saw no reason to wake from it. Except for that nasty asteroid business.

The group entered the restaurant and were directed to a private dining room by a dapper man who greeted David warmly as if they had been friends for a long time. They saw the extensive buffet that had been set up with various styles of food and wine that was far in excess of what eight people could possibly eat.

"I tried to pick a wide assortment of food based on your eclectic tastes. I thought buffet style would be best so we could talk in private and not be interrupted by servers. Please feel free to help yourselves and eat up. I don't get a refund for uneaten food," David said with a smile.

Slowly at first, the group eventually lined up for food and a wide variety of Riesling, Chardonnay, Sauvignon Blanc, and Pinot Grigio wines. As they feasted on lobster, shrimp, swordfish, and grouper, they finally loosened up with the help of the wine and talked in whispered voices during dinner. There was even some nervous laughter.

When dinner was finished, David directed them to another room. "Please come this way for some after-dinner drinks and dessert. They have terrific apple pie here."

After entering the rustic room featuring a huge fireplace, an exposed wood-beam ceiling, and flagstone floor, the group sat around a huge two-hundred-year-old oak table. They sipped cognac and coffee then partook of the as-advertised great apple pie.

After all the food, wine, and conversation, there was an air of anticipation as they waited for David, who was engaged in an earnest discussion with Stephan over the plight of the LA Dodgers. It was Abir who began the formal proceedings with a question.

"Okay, David, you've definitely made your point about who you are and what you are. But why the hell are we all here, and what do you want from us?"

CHAPTER 14

"AS I SAID BACK IN ASPEN, the Earth, well, is pretty much fucked, is the best way I can say it. Every life form will be turned to ash in less than a year unless you seven convince the rest of the world to change. But more importantly, you need to convince the Congress of Planets, the group I represent, that the change will be permanent."

"Well, that's a pretty succinct explanation," Stephan said.

"No time to be oblique," David said.

"First of all, David, what is the Congress of Planets?" Robert asked.

"It's sort of like your United Nations, except it's made up of intelligent beings."

"You said we have to change. Change to what? And for what? If everyone is going to die in a year anyway, why change anything at this point?" Billy asked.

"The people I report to have the ability to save Earth, but there is no point in doing that since you're killing it as surely as that asteroid will."

"How could you save Earth?" Robert asked.

"Simple—we just vaporize the asteroid in deep space millions of miles from Earth, as we've done hundreds of times before, and bingo, the Earth is saved by the good guys."

"You said you've done this before?" Mei asked.

"Dr. Liu, I'd think you, of all people, would question why Mars and your moon have been hit with thousands of asteroids, yet Earth has had no significant asteroid hits in recorded history. Do you think Earth was just lucky?"

"Why would your planet protect Earth?" Stephan asked.

"We don't think of it in terms of us protecting Earth or any specific planet. Rather, we are among a group of numerous cultures that banded together over a thousand years ago to protect life in all forms. At that time, we agreed to protect new and evolving civilizations like yours by virtue of our technologies. Sort of like when you guys protect an endangered species here on Earth. Or when you try to help the whales when they come too close to shore and get trapped by a low tide. It's just the right thing to do."

"But if that's the case, why wouldn't you protect us now?" Mei asked.

"Because by your collective behaviors, you're killing a planet you have no right to kill. Plus, eventually you're going to kill virtually every living thing on it. So, if you're going to do it anyway over the next hundred years, it may as well happen next year when Big Ben makes a visit. Why waste our time? Eventually, Earth will regrow itself, and a new life form will develop that perhaps won't be so damn arrogant," David said calmly.

"David, have you shared our history with the folks?" José asked.

"No, I thought that would be a story told best by you, José."

"Okay. A few years ago, David came up to me on a sidewalk in Rome and introduced himself. He said he had some things he wanted to share with me, including that he was a visitor from another damn planet and a bunch of other crazy stuff. I thought he was full of shit."

"Not the first time I'd heard that," David said.

"Anyway, among the many things David told me was that organized religion on Earth was a hoax and what we define as our God, and all the other all gods on Earth, are myths. He also explained how organized religion is nothing but big business. Its product is false hope, and it takes in billions of dollars each year selling that product. And how religion has been the genesis, no pun intended, for endless wars and suffering, over hundreds, even thousands of years."

"You believed that crap, Father?" John asked.

"Please, call me José. No, not at first, John. But then David was able to share some incredible things with me that made me understand that what we consider..."

"Understand what? That some guy with a Corvette that flies shows up and you turn your back on thousands of years of faith and the Word of God? What about the billions of people that believe in religion? You think they're all crazy?" John asked.

"He's not saying religion does no good on Earth, because it does. But we should focus on helping each other out of a respect for humanity, not because of a collection of false deities," José said.

"Tell you the truth, I think all religion's bullshit no matter what church you're talking about. So if David here has a better story to tell, I'd listen," Billy said.

"When I was president, it was understood you had to project an image of being religious to even be considered for any public office. It was a rite of passage whether you really believed or not. The public demanded that their president, at least on the surface, believe in some kind of religion."

"That sounds like a typical bullshit politician statement, Mr. President, Bob, sir. C'mon, man, are you a believer or not?" Billy asked.

"No, I'm not and never have been. But I would have never been elected president if I had said that in public."

"You are all just a bunch of damn atheists," John said.

"So are you, John," Billy said with a laugh.

"The hell I am. I believe in God and always will, don't you be callin' me a damn atheist or there's gonna be trouble."

"John, there are about twenty so-called organized religions in the world, and another 250 branches of those major groups. Almost everyone has some form of god or Supreme Being. You don't believe in those other gods worshipped by billions of people around the world, and neither do I, so in that way we are both atheists to all those other gods. The difference between you and me is I don't believe in your God either," Billy said.

John glared at Billy.

"David, I'm confused. What does any religion, whether you are a believer or not, have to do with an asteroid destroying Earth?" Mei asked.

"Nothing, directly, Mei. But it has everything to do with how Earth is managed going forward. *If* you go forward. You guys live in insular worlds of ignorance and stupidity. You form self-indulgent, self-serving, petty global alliances, all based on money, power, and ego, which certainly includes organized religion, politics, and governments. All those things have incredibly negative impacts on the people of Earth, and ultimately on the physical planet itself."

"David, I see your points and for the most part agree, but in reality, how can you legislate how people think or in what they believe? Robert asked. "Even if organized religion was somehow banned, people would hang on to their beliefs. I know from personal experience that in many cases it is their only hope and comfort in lives filled with abject misery and want."

"Did you ever think about eliminating the abject misery and want, Robert?" David asked.

"It's not that easy," José said.

"Sure it is. Your church has a net worth of a half a trillion dollars, tax free I might add. All the other religions combined around the world have even more. Yet last year, eight million people died of starvation on your planet, while you guys were paying out millions in law suit money for things we won't talk about here, bought new robes for your cardinals, and built some really cool condos for your archbishops in Vatican City. At the same time, Muslims shelled out nearly a billion dollars to build twenty new mosques and retreats around the world. What the fuck is that all about?" David asked.

"Okay, I get it. But you still can't stop people from believing, no matter what you say or do. History has proved that, José maintained.

"I agree that's true in the short term. But atheism is the fastest growing group in your world today. People are finally understanding that organized religion is all bullshit. I understand the believing part, but if organized religion is eliminated, people will, over time, forget about all the dogma and the ridiculous trappings that go with it. They will begin to believe in something else. Something far bigger. Something real. Something universal. They will eventually understand that believing in humanity, including sharing with one another, is far better than sending cash to an organization that has a greater net worth than the combined value of the top ten Fortune companies in the world."

"That sounds like nothing more than communism on a vast scale,

David," Robert said.

"I am not saying there wouldn't be recognition of individual talent, creativity, and hard work—there would be. But with no organized religion, no borders around countries, and no leaders to hoard wealth, the Earth would in essence become one country, one people, that would share the Earth's resources, its medical discoveries, its food, its water, its air, everything."

"The nearly three hundred countries around the world would never agree to open borders. They value their sovereignty, their history, their identity, their flag, and the protection their borders provide," the former president said.

"You mean if the borders between Mexico, the United States, Canada and the twenty other countries that make up North America were erased, that there would somehow be chaos or internal upheaval?"

"People would be very upset and…"

"Robert, the people wouldn't be upset, it's the leaders of those countries that would be upset. They would fear a loss of power and control. Governments exist to enrich their leaders and rule over a powerless working class," David said calmly.

For several minutes, the room was quiet, as David's words began to sink in. It took some time for the enormity of what he was asking the group to do began to coalesce into a shared, hopeless, even frightening thought.

"And you think the seven of us can do anything to fix things like religion or geographic boundaries, or all those other problems you mentioned? In a year? If so, David, forgive me for saying so, but even though you may be intergalactic, you are also completely delusional," Mei said.

"Mei, all I can say is, you guys better fix the problems."

CHAPTER 15

DAVID'S WORDS HUNG IN THE AIR, and the group again grew quiet and uncomfortable. Former president Mitchell got up and poured a glass of wine. He walked around the table and moved to a window that overlooked a beautiful flower garden and gently flowing creek both illuminated by the last sliver of a setting sun.

"The incongruity and the enormity of all this may be just a bit too much for us to comprehend. Here we are having drinks with what we'd call an alien and are told if we don't change fundamental aspects of life on Earth in the course of a year, our planet will be destroyed."

"Would you rather wake up in a year and be incinerated an hour after your morning corn flakes and coffee?" David asked.

José looked around the room and said, "Look, when I first heard all this, I felt the same way you guys are feeling now. But since then, I've learned and seen things I never dreamed of. It was my idea to contact all of you to see if there was something we could do. What David is presenting is a chance for us to not only save the physical Earth, but to reshape life on the Earth. To create a world that most of us would refer to as something close to heaven—a heaven right here on Earth."

"Say what, José? I thought David just said there ain't no heaven. Now there is?" John asked.

"John, you and I have been preaching and believing things that don't exist. But it doesn't mean they can't exist if we build them."

"Only God can invite us to heaven, the real heaven; it's not something we all can just build. That wouldn't be heaven; that would be a make-believe Disneyland Heaven or some such thing."

"John, how do you perceive an afterlife? What is your idea of heaven, exactly?" David asked.

John thought for a moment and sat back in his chair. "It's a place where there's no evil, no hunger, people are free, people are happy, and you see all your friends and relatives that have passed on. Even see your old dogs. It's always sunny and…there's music and there's no pain from your past. That's my heaven."

"Except for no baseball, that sounds like a pretty good place, John," David said. "The funny thing is, some people in the universe have been living that way for thousands of years."

John looked at David for several moments but said nothing.

Leaving his chair and pouring a glass of scotch, Abir said, "This is absurd. You want the seven of us to rebuild societies, cultures, religions, geopolitical structures, and fundamental belief systems in a year, after it took thousands of years and billions of people to build what we have now. Anyone who believes that can happen is fucking crazy," Amir said.

Stephan rose from his seat and walked to a fruit bowl and grabbed a handful of grapes. "Frankly, I don't give a shit if Earth is turned into ash or not. I have terminal liver cancer, and I'll be dead this time next year before Big Ben blows this place to shit. But I am curious about lots of things, David, and if you have such insight into religion, maybe you have answers to questions I've always wondered about."

"Yeah, I probably do. But for everyone's information, the cancer Stephan has didn't form in his liver. It started as a blood cancer that his liver took the brunt of; eventually, the cancer took over his entire body. By the way, Stephan, given the current rapid growth of the cancer cells in your body, you'll be dead in three months, so you may want to give up flying sooner than later."

"How the hell you know this stuff?" Stephan asked.

"Because we gave you the cancer, Stephan," David said.

When they heard David's words, a collective jolt of fear moved through the group like an electric current. At first they gaped at David but then looked at Stephan, who appeared unmoved by what he had just heard.

"Sure you did," Stephan said casually with a half-laugh, as he stuffed two more large green grapes into his mouth.

"Would you like to see your X-rays? I have them on my iPad," David said.

"You gave Stephan cancer? Why and how would you do such a thing?" Robert asked.

"The how was easy. We subjected the ten cases of bottled water he keeps in his house to radioactivity. By the time he was through the fifth case, he'd ingested enough radiation to kill an elephant," David explained.

"That water was in a closet in my kitchen... how did...?"

"Look guys, we came here over a thousand years ago from a galaxy far, far away. You think we'd have a problem getting into Stephan's house in Bel Air? C'mon, give us some credit."

"You didn't say why you gave Stephan cancer," Mei said.

"Oh yeah. Well, that's the cool part; we gave Stephan cancer so we could cure him and provide you guys some of the proof we knew you were going to ask for. You know, that miracle type bullshit you folks love so much. You guys do love your miracles."

"My cancer has metastasized from my liver to every organ in my body."

"It's also in your bones, skin, and gonads. You're a dead man walking and flying, Stevie boy."

"And you can cure him?" Robert asked.

"Sure we can. We began curing cancer when you guys were still living in caves and howling at the moon."

"How?" Billy asked.

"How? Because we know shit," David said as he reached into his pocket and pulled out a small glass vial that contained a liquid that had an iridescent purple glow. "This stuff will provide a total cure of your cancer—not remission mind you, but a total cure, in a day."

David tossed the vial to Stephan, who dropped it onto the stone floor. The vial bounced several times on the polished rock but didn't break.

"We also perfected unbreakable glass some time ago as well," David said with pride.

Stephan picked up the vial and stared at its contents for nearly a minute, a small grin on his face.

"It's not poison, is it?" Stephan asked.

"Are you fucking kidding me, Stephan? Why would we poison a dead man? You guys are really incredibly stupid sometimes. Just drink what the fuck is inside, and your cancer is gone, and it will never come back. By the way, it'll fix that irregular heartbeat you got too. I threw that in for no extra charge, along with a real good vitamin supplement that will last the rest of your life, which will now be quite a bit longer in duration and quality—potentially."

Stephan opened the vial and sniffed its contents. His small grin grew wider until it was a full-fledged teeth-exposing smile.

"You ain't really gonna drink that stuff, are you?" John asked.

Without answering, Stephan swigged down the contents in the vial. "Tastes like grape juice." He said.

"I tried to get the aged scotch flavor but couldn't find it," David said with a tone of apology.

Stephan sat down in his chair and was quiet for several moments as the rest of the group stared at him waiting for a reaction. His wide smile widened even more.

"C'mon people. I said it will take a day before he's cured. Damn, give it a chance." David said. "Let's move on."

While he continued to glance sideways at Stephan looking for the instantaneous cancer cure, Billy asked, "SETI has been sending out signals to every corner of the galaxy for decades. Why haven't we heard any response from your group or any other civilization?" Billy asked.

"We've been intercepting your signals because there are some folks out there you really don't want to come for a nice neighborly visit."

"What do you mean?"

"I mean not every planet or civilization is inhabited by beings that play well with others. If they hear your signal and are in the mood, they might show up some day, kill every living being on Earth in an hour just for kicks, and move on to the next planet for lunch. Like when you guys kill a colony of ants in your backyard for the hell of it."

"That kind of power exists?" Mei asked.

"Oh yeah, it exists. But it's not just the power, it's the belief you guys are no more than pests that should be whacked for the good of the universe."

"Why haven't you guys come in and taken us over before now?" Billy asked.

"We're part of an organization of planets that banded together a couple thousand years ago. We believe each planet and its civilizations have the right to develop at their own pace as long as they don't threaten other planets or their own. When they do, we can—and do—step in."

"Was our development of nuclear weapons a problem for you guys?" Robert asked.

"Not really, at least not from us defending ourselves from you guys. Your weapons are no match for what we possess. But they can mess up the planet for a good long while if you started nuking each other for fun and profit."

"If you are really from another planet...?"

"See, Abir, there's that doubt in your voice again, that, 'if you are really from another planet,' bullshit. That's why it's hard to get you guys engaged. You always question, doubt, and ignore reality. Ignore facts. Hell, you even ignore math. I'm from another planet, get over it. It's really that not a big deal. Do you really think that in all the universes—yeah, there's more than one—you are the only planet with microwave ovens, cable TV, or ice cream? Look, I'm trying to save your collective asses, but you really need to work with me here."

"I believe what you're saying, David. I saw secret reports when I was in office of alien landings and even contact with beings. But the reports said they didn't look like you," Robert said.

"Yeah, they are what you guys call the "Grays," "Reptilians," or "Nordics," among others, are really just androids on reconnaissance missions. They're harmless."

"How many civilizations have come to Earth to check us out?" Mei asked.

"Hard to say, but a bunch. A hundred or so, I guess," David said.

"Why do you look like us?" Billy asked.

"We don't. You look like us. At least some of us. My group first came here about 20,000 years ago looking for natural resources and encountered your predecessors. They were strong but not too bright compared to other civilizations in the universe, but we needed labor to do some mining. So, we added some of our DNA to your ancestors to jump-start the evolution process. Over a few thousand years, your ancestors got smarter, and we got the workforce we needed that eventually evolved into you guys. Over time we added more of our DNA so you ended up looking similar to us. You know, it allowed us to kind of blend."

"I don't believe in evolution. There is no proof that...,"Abir said.

"Abir, please, there you are being a dick again, and we don't have time for you to be a dick. You're not on the idiot box now talking to a bunch of fundamentalist nut jobs with third- grade educations. Evolution is a basic law of science, not a topic to be debated by people capable of reading a fucking book. C'mon, man, get over yourself, it's time to move on."

Abir started to argue but instead he sat down, took a large drink of bourbon, and stared out the window.

"David has shown me what I feel is proof of things that, beyond question, I never dreamed possible. Proof that we will need to convey to seven billion people over the next year to convince them we need to change or pay the consequences. But even without the asteroid, we have a chance to bring our world together and create a new age of humankind, José said.

"José, that's impossible and you know it. It's hard to get seven people to agree on anything, let alone seven billion," Billy said.

David rose from his chair and began walking around the room. "Billy, we've learned it depends on what you show them and what you tell them. Ironically, it's the less educated that are the easiest to convince of a new way to live and a new approach to life. The highly educated are much harder to get to accept new ideas because they like the way things are now. In many cases, they believe they know more than they really do. Based on that false assumption, they live with blinders on; they won't even consider a change even though their lives would be far better than they can imagine. Plus, the wealthy and educated are far more dangerous."

"More dangerous?" Mei asked.

"Yes. The more educated will say one thing and do another, you know, like politicians. That's dangerous for you guys, my folks, and the Earth," David said.

For several moments, the group sat in silence and tried to comprehend everything they had heard from David over a four-hour period. Some couldn't comprehend and never would.

"So, what now?" Robert asked wearily.

"Look, you guys have had a lot thrown at you over a few hours. Let's head back to the house, get some rest, and pick things up tomorrow. Okay?" David suggested.

The group nodded in unison and slowly filed out of the restaurant, leaving David alone.

"Don't worry, I got the tip," David said as he pulled out his American Express Black Card.

CHAPTER 16

BACK INSIDE THE CRAFT, THE group returned to their previous position at the front near David, who held the ship's control mechanism in his hand. "How about if we take a little detour back to Aspen? It won't take long," he suggested.

The craft rose two thousand feet into the air and turned toward the west instead of east toward Aspen. David pushed a button, and the craft disappeared into the horizon where it chased down a setting sun. Darkness gave way to light.

In less than seven minutes after it passed over the coast of California, the Hawaiian Islands could be seen then gone. Several minutes more and the coast of China appeared then slipped beneath the craft in a multicolored blur.

After David turned southeast, he guided the craft over India and then the Arabian Sea. Within seconds he slowed down the speed of the craft as it passed over Central Africa. He came down to near ground level and sped across Ethiopia, Sudan, Chad, Niger, Mali before exploding past the African coastline and into the darkness once again.

Within a minute the East Coast of the United States was visible, then in less than four minutes later they hovered five thousand feet above Denver.

"We could have gone faster, but you would have missed some sights," David said to a group who had no words left to utter.

After David secured the craft, he led the group single file back to the house in what appeared to be an aggregation of the disbelieving. They all knew it had really happened, but their brains couldn't accept what their eyes had seen and their senses had felt. They knew instinctively that this marked the beginning of their new world or the ending of their old world. Or both.

In an effort to snap his guests out of their collective shock, David asked, "Anyone for a nightcap? I have a pretty nice selection of domestic reds and Italian whites if you're interested."

After getting no takers from the group who had for some reason gathered in the kitchen, Robert finally said, "I think we all need a good night's sleep after today. I know I do." The others nodded in unison.

"I understand. You all go get some rest, and we'll pick things up in the morning. Your names are on the bedroom doors, and each room has its own bathroom and TV. If you need anything, just yell. Goodnight all."

After the group headed to their respective rooms, David was alone in the kitchen. He grabbed a cold beer, picked up his cell, and dialed. "Hi. Yeah, it went okay. I should be home Monday night unless, well, you know, as long as things don't blow up here. Okay. See ya."

David tossed his phone on the couch, stretched, yawned, and then went to his room leaving the downstairs area empty. After a few moments, the lights in the house went out and the glow from a full silver moon filtered into the darkened house.

CHAPTER 17

FROM HIS UPSTAIRS BEDROOM WINDOW, Father José Manuel Francisco Alberto Peña could almost feel the light from the full moon on his bare chest. He looked out at the beauty of the mountains and knew his decision to try to save Earth was really the only decision he could have made. To lose things like he was seeing at that moment, or worse, to lose everything that had ever been created for all time by all the billions of people who had built civilization, was not truly an option. If only two people were left, it would be worth it. "We could just start over," he whispered to himself.

Growing up in Cuba, he eventually realized he had limited opportunities there. While he always dreamed of moving to America and joining Carlos Santana on tour as his rhythm guitarist, he realized by age thirteen that may have been a longshot dream, since there was no way he could get to the U.S. or Mexico to meet Carlos and couldn't yet play guitar. In fact, he had never owned a guitar.

But he could sing, well enough to join the choir at the Lady of Mercy Church outside Havana, where his group would regularly perform in front of the Cuban Bishop's Conference. When he was seventeen, his choir received an invitation from the Vatican to attend the Easter ceremony in Vatican Square and join choirs from around the world for Easter Mass.

The trip changed José's life. First of all, he learned he liked to fly and was shocked at the free food they all got during the flight. He learned he loved Rome. He loved its beauty, its people, (especially the shapely women), its food, its history. All of it.

When the time neared to return to Cuba, José did not want to go. He thought of defecting, but he knew that surviving in a strange country without a job, money, or a place to live was nearly impossible. He thought of going to the Italian government but feared he would be deported and his already difficult life in Cuba would be even worse for him and his family.

Finally, on the day before his scheduled departure, he went to a bishop at the Vatican who served as a valet and confidant for a cardinal and told him that he wanted to stay in Italy. "Are you prepared to serve God?" he was asked.

Hell yes he thought, if it meant staying in Italy. "Yes, Father, I am."

"Life is different here," he was told.

No shit. "Yes Father, I know and I want to serve God in any way I can."

"Let me talk to the cardinal and tell him your wishes."

You do that, my man. "Thank you, Father."

After receiving a visa to remain in Italy with the recommendation of the Vatican, José finished his high school education then entered a monastery in Tuscany. After graduating,, he was assigned to the Vatican and worked in low-level administrative jobs for the next ten years.

Even before he met David, José had his issues with the Catholic Church. All the money, the politics, the bureaucracy, the political in-fighting between and among men of God made him question it all. How could this happen in the Church he had grown to love? Why not just focus on the people? Give them hope that one day things would be better. Hell, just give them money to eat and to live if they needed it. He had asked that question many times and never received a satisfactory answer.

Venturing out in "civilian" clothes on a Saturday afternoon in Siena for some sight- seeing, José was having lunch, including an excellent Cabernet Sauvignon, when a middle- aged man sat down uninvited at his table and asked, "How's the wine, Padré?"

Over the next several hours, David and José talked, debated, laughed, got angry, ate, drank a considerable amount of wine, and by the end of the day had become friends. Then David had to go and fuck it up when told he José he was an alien. No, not from another country. A little further away than that. Not surprisingly, José told David he was full of shit.

"You're full of shit."

"Let's go take a ride."

After returning from a circumnavigation of Earth in less than an hour, José had a new best friend with a real cool ride. But he also found someone with whom he could communicate and tell him what he felt about things. Over a three-year period David told him about Big Ben and his plans to save the world. "What do you think of my plans?"

"Remember when I said you were full of shit?"

"Yeah, I remember."

"Well, you're also crazy. People on Earth would never go for such an idea even if it meant saving the planet."

"Then everything will be destroyed."

"Let me think about it," José said.

After several days, José contacted David and suggested a group of people to be part of a sort of an ad hoc committee. The group came from a list of possibilities that David had already prepared and shown to José to get his input.

That first group failed. So did the second and third. "One more and I'm done," David said.

José had a good feeling about this last group. They represented a diverse population segment, were smart, and he thought they could be convinced to do what needed to be done. He hoped he was right.

CHAPTER 18

DR. MEI LIU WALKED ONTO the large deck wearing an MIT sweatshirt, sweatpants, and tennis shoes. She saw Stephan already sitting at the table with a cup of hot coffee grasped in both hands. The early morning sun was barely visible in the eastern sky, yet it cast a golden haze over the trees that cascaded down the slope. " And I thought I was an early riser," she said.

"Morning. Sure is beautiful out here this time of day. Want some coffee? I brought the pot out with me."

"Sure, thanks. I'm almost afraid to ask this, but do you feel any change in your condition?"

Stephan poured Mei a cup of coffee.

"I had lumps the size of golf balls under my arms, in my groin, and along my rib cage yesterday. They were all gone this morning."

"Oh my God, Stephan. That's wonderful news. I couldn't be happier."

"Yeah, pretty cool. After having this death thing hanging over my head for so long, I forgot what it's like to feel normal again. Like a lot of folks, there were years where I took living for granted. I won't ever do that again."

"Do you think David would release the stuff he gave you to the rest of the world?"

"I don't know, but it would be a great tool to get people to come over to our side if he did."

"Have you actually picked a side yet?"

"If everything David told us last night about the asteroid is true, and you said it was, I'm not sure there is much of a choice to be made here. Not to be overly dramatic, but the way I see it, the entire history and future of man is at stake."

"I think you're right. The information he gave us about the asteroid was accurate. But how we address it with seven billion other people on the planet is another story completely," Mei said.

"What David told us last night is arguably the most important information that has ever been given to the human race. This is not a situation where we should try to gain a consensus; we simply need to act in the best interest of civilization."

"How do we define 'best interests' for the rest of a civilization, a planet? I already see differences of opinion in our group of seven."

"Well, we better come up with a plan quick, or curing cancer will give people a lot of false hope that they're going to lead long lives," Stephan said.

"I'm afraid you're right."

For several minutes Mei and Stephan stared in silence at the pine tree-covered mountains being bathed in a now brighter yellow by a rising sun.

"It would appear at some point you had a tough career decision to make."

"Career decision?" Mei asked.

"Yeah, astrophysicist or Victoria's Secret model."

Mei laughed at Stephan's comment. "To tell you the truth, I did some modeling in New York to help pay for college and was tempted by the money. But I guess I was just too curious about the world around me."

"Where are you from?"

"I was born in Beijing but adopted at an early age. Never knew my real parents. My adoptive parents told me I needed to come to this country for my education. So when I turned twelve, I was sent here to study."

"You came here alone, at twelve?"

"Yes, my parents were college professors and could not leave their posts without the risk of losing their jobs."

"Wow. Twelve and you went to another country? Could you even speak the language over here?"

"I was fluent in English and that helped. But I was lonely in the private schools and missed my parents very much."

"That must have been very tough on you."

"Being alone made me focus on my studies. And eventually I made friends and things got better."

"Did you get back home much?"

"Once a year for a month I went back to China. I missed my family and my country, but over time it got easier. My life is here now."

"How about a husband, two and half kids, a van, and a home in suburbia?"

"Maybe someday, but based on what David told us, maybe not," Mei said.

The sliding door to the house opened and José, Billy, John, Abir, and Robert came onto the deck all with various degrees of sleeplessness etched on their faces.

"Morning, everyone," Mei said.

"Morning. Wow, what a view," Billy said.

"Who wants coffee?" Stephan asked as he held up the large glass coffee pot and pointed to the cups, creamers, and sugar he had brought out from the kitchen.

Stephan got up and began pouring cups of coffee for the rest of the group.

"Gentlemen, I have wonderful news. Stephan just told me the lumps he had all over his body yesterday were gone this morning, " Mei announced.

"I'll be damned! Congratulations, Stephan, I'm very happy for you." Robert said.

"The morning does seem a bit brighter than it has for a while after waking up and feeling those golf balls inside me gone." Stephan said.

"I'm glad those lumps are gone, but I couldn't sleep last night thinkin' about what David said about God and the church. Ain't no way I can go back to my people and tell them everything they believe in is a damn lie, even if I got all the proof in the world."

As John spoke, David stumbled onto the deck in an old bathrobe. He had some serious "pillow hair" and appeared in desperate need of coffee or hair of the dog. Whichever was closest...and quickest.

"Too much red wine last night. I feel like shit," David announced to the group with sincerity.

"Here, have a cup," Stephan handed David a cup of coffee.

"Thanks, Stephan. Are your lumps gone?" David asked.

"Yeah, they're gone. Thanks, I think."

"No problem. Sorry to put you through all that medical stuff, but I needed to make a point with you and the rest of these folks."

"What would've happened if I didn't make this trip?"

"We would have snuck the cure into your food or water at some point, but I figured you'd show up. If not, you would have probably shown up on the cover of the *National Enquirer* as part of their "Miracle Cure" series. Bit more dramatic this way, don't you think?"

"Glad to help. Actually gave me a much better perspective on life in general. I think I'll appreciate things a bit more now and in the future, assuming any of us has a future. What are the chances of getting that medicine to the rest of the world?" Stephan said.

"Not good, at least now."

"Why not?"

"Mainly because nearly 10 million people around the world will die this year from cancer."

"What? I don't understand," Billy said.

"If those ten million people lived, they'd generate about two billion people in a few generations. You guys need cancer, heart disease, and AIDS, along with a few wars and natural disasters, to keep populations in check."

"You can't be serious?" Mei asked.

"Sure I am."

"What about your concern for all those starving people you said the church ain't feeding? What's the difference?" John asked.

"Not feeding people is murder. Not curing people is nature taking its course. Besides, at least in this country, cancer patients are living longer and longer and in far better conditions than destitute people who are forced to watch their starving babies die in their arms," David said.

"Sorry, I don't see much of a difference either," Stephan said.

"Look, population is one of the things we need to discuss today, but before we get into all that, how about I make some French toast and sausage for everyone?"

CHAPTER 19

THE GROUP ATE BREAKFAST PREPARED by David on the deck that overlooked the vista of the Rocky Mountains. They talked, laughed, and ate, despite a feeling of shared angst over what David had alluded to before the meal. It was as if the group did not want to hear the rest of what David had to say about population.

After breakfast, it was Abir who finally raised the issue. "David, what did you mean when you said something about keeping the population in check?"

David had donned his favorite Wayfarer sunglasses, the ones with the blue-tinted lenses, and looked up into the sun as he lay back on his favorite cushioned lounger. He responded to Abir nonchalantly. "One of the many things my people are going to need to see is a reduction in Earth's population."

"Reduction?" Robert asked. "Don't you mean stabilization or zero growth?"

"No, I'm talking reduction. There are way too many people on Earth given its resources. Sort of like the deficit spending that Americans are all about. It's real simple; if there is not a reduction in population, everyone dies on this planet, one way or the other. Ergo, population *reduction,* not stabilization or zero growth, is definitely required."

Several of the group laughed at David's off-hand comment. They then looked at each one another nervously, as if to say, "He's kidding, right?"

"There are over seven billion people on earth today and the population increases around 2 percent a year. Using the Rule of 72, the population will be fifteen billion in less than forty years," Robert explained.

"Given Big Ben's pending visit, I really wouldn't worry about what happens in forty years," David said as he continued to bask in the sun.

"What are you talking about, David?" Abir asked.

"There's no way this planet can support its current population, much less fifteen billion in forty years, or fifty billion in a hundred years. No fucking way."

"If you and your associates would nuke that rock, I'd take our chances," Abir said.

"Why bother? Every person on earth will die in a hundred years anyway. Not only that, but before a hundred years comes, people will start dropping dead from lack of oxygen, water, and food. It won't be pretty."

"David, perhaps you're used to dealing with higher intellect life forms, but I have an IQ of 171 and I can't figure out what the hell you want from us," Mei said.

David removed his shades and took a sip of iced tea. "Mei, my IQ is around 230 and I'm somewhere in the fiftieth percentile of my peer group. One of my sons was tested at 255, and he's nine. We are in fact much smarter than you individually and the human race generally, and as a result, we feel an obligation to try to save your collective asses and planet, if we can. It's like that example I gave of you guys trying to save pilot whales trapped in shallow water. You try to save them because, like I said before, it's the right thing to do."

"Are you saying the relative difference in our intelligence to you, is the difference between us and whales?" Billy asked.

"Actually, given all your built-in prejudices, beliefs, and lack of worldwide education that collectively keeps a lid on human intellectual development, you're closer to the whales than to us."

"So what? So you're smarter than us and have fancier airplanes, what the hell does that mean?" John asked.

"It means that for a few thousand years, you guys have not developed as we had hoped. You are, for the most part, a generally intellectually disabled group, compared to the rest of those in the nearby cosmos. And now, you are fucking up the planet you live on. Based on all that, you guys have some tough decisions to make."

"Like what?" John said.

"Like do you want a big rock the size of Cincinnati to melt your planet in a year, or do you want to make some changes and join the rest of the universe in some good living? Your choice."

"If it means tellin' my people there ain't no God and that everything they believed all their lives ain't true, then to hell with the Earth and to hell with you. We'll all die together and meet in heaven."

"Wow, that's an enlightened position to take. Wonder how the whales would respond?" David asked.

John edged toward and then hovered over David as he conversed with him. David remained seated and calmly took another sip of iced tea.

"Father Peña, I mean, José, is there a heaven?" David asked.

"I used to think so. But now I'm not sure what I thought makes sense anymore."

"Do any of you really believe in what most organized religions on this planet call or define as a 'Heaven'? You know the golden streets, the angels, the harp, all that nonsense?" David asked.

"I think there's something there when you die. I'm not sure what, but something," Abir said.

"None of you believe that shit. You're too smart, even you, John. You're just a good man telling people you care about what they want to hear," David said flatly.

"Do you know what happens when we die, David?" Stephan asked in a tone that seemed he was afraid to hear the answer.

"Stephan, you die. You just die. There's no heaven. No afterlife, no golden streets, but so what? Can you remember what it was like before you were born? That is what it's like after you die. Nothing. Nothing at all."

"David, even if you are right and I think you might be, that will be a depressing and even terrifying thought for many religious people. Even if we don't believe in things like a heaven, people need hope that things will be better for them," José said. "Even if it's not true, there is no need to take away that hope."

"José, false hope given to hopeless people is a shit sandwich and a cruel device to keep the masses in line. Make them all kinds of promises for a so-called heaven when they die, so they won't rise up from the hell they live in and cause problems. That's religion," Billy said.

"But isn't that enough? Why take away their hope just to prove we can?" José countered.

"David, how can you know what happens when we die?" Mei asked.

"Thousands of years ago our scientists discovered that death was final in its termination of life. There is no brain cognition, no sensory activity; you simply cease to exist. So as a culture we determined that the key to replacing the concept of an afterlife was to greatly enhance the quality of existing life. To defer death until the living person decided they'd lived long enough and ended their life by their own volition.

"Who would do such a thing?" Billy asked.

"A person who had lived five or six hundred years and experienced everything there is to experience and was simply tired of living, that's who." David said.

"If no one dies, how do you control birth rates or population rates?" Mei asked.

"Ever hear of the pill? Or how about people getting licenses to have children. In our societies, you must qualify to have children. There's an application and qualification process. You know, sort of like you guys have to qualify to drive a car or adopt a pet from a shelter. What a concept," David said sarcastically.

"Sounds Orwellian," Stephan said.

"No, it's common sense, thoughtful logic, and a consideration of the people already living and a recognition of the resources available to provide for our people," David explained. "If millions of people are starving on Earth today, does it make sense to have millions more born into such a brutal circumstance?"

"How does no God and no afterlife impact your societies? Is there more murder or crime?" Abir asked.

"We have virtually no crime. There is no need for crime. Everyone has everything they want based on their needs and desires. At birth, each person has a chip imbedded in their brain that makes it impossible for them to kill another person."

"What about wars?" Robert asked.

"Our planets, or the civilizations on those planets, do not fight among themselves because there are no boundaries, thus nothing to fight over. But like I said, there are some bad dudes out there in the universes that like nothing better than to take over a civilization for fun and profit. So we stay well-armed to make sure we protect ourselves."

After he had stared down at him for several minutes with a scowl on his face, John reached out and swatted David's glass of iced tea from his hand. It slammed against the wall of house and exploded into a thousand pieces.

CHAPTER 20

JOHN'S VOICE WAS RAW WITH emotion as he raged at David, "I've heard enough of this blasphemy! No God, no heaven, havin' babies with chips put in 'em! I ain't havin' it! And neither are my people. I'm leavin' and I'm tellin' the world what you want us to do and..."

Aside from an almost imperceptible smile on his face, David didn't respond in any way to John's outburst. Instead, he slowly got up from his chair, went to the table, and poured himself another glass of iced tea. "John, please sit down," David said softly while he looked directly into John's eyes.

"I said I'm leavin'..."

"No, you're not, John. Not now anyway, and if you do, you won't tell anyone anything about what you saw or heard here. Not ever."

In spite of himself, John felt compelled to sit down. He became quiet as if detecting the slightest threat in David's voice. Or was it something else he responded to? Something unheard and unseen but something felt and understood.

"Folks, let me explain something as simply as I can. You were invited here to help save your planet. Whether you do or don't is up to you. Since I've been living here a long time, I kind of like the place and hope you do the right thing. But in the end, it's entirely up to you."

"David, what you're asking is impossible. You told us you have lived on this planet for years; if so, you must know that I'm right. Seven people, no matter who they are, can't make seven billion people agree on anything," Robert said.

"That's what the previous groups said."

The seven looked at each other, confused. "Previous groups?" Stephan asked.

"You're the fourth group we've brought in and you'll be the last. Go ahead, ask José."

José nodded to the group and said, "Yep, he's right."

"How come we haven't heard anything from the other three?" Robert asked.

"Because once they determine they can't or won't work on the project, I cleanse their memories, and they have no recollection of anything they've heard or seen. I'll do the same with you guys."

"But the Bible says...," John said in a whisper.

"John, who the hell do you think wrote your Bible? You guys were a bunch of thick- headed slugs who barely walked upright and, in some cases, thought fire was magic, even after we gave you some of our DNA. The Bible was a set of rules that we hoped would keep you guys from killing each other long enough till you all grew up. Unfortunately, we're still waiting."

"You guys wrote our Bible? I don't believe a damn word..."

In a tone of understanding, David said, "I know you don't, John, and I completely understand how you feel. But how you feel is no longer the issue. The truth is the truth, no matter who believes it. But it was our hope that by getting someone like you on the team, you could help convince those who follow your teachings that organized religion has been one of the root causes of much of the misery over the millennia. This includes wars, torture, famine, and already irreparable damage to Earth. Until boundaries around countries, organized religions, political cabals and other global issues are addressed, your civilization will inevitably kill itself, and will do so very quickly. More importantly, you could in the process also kill the planet, and that is something we will not allow."

Staggered by his words, John turned away from David and stared out into the dense grouping of pine trees that lined the ski slope far into the distance. The rest of the group sat in silence moving their eyes from David to John, unclear of what to do or say next.

Finally, Stephan said, "John, I know this is tough for you, but it sounds like you can be part of the problem or part of the solution."

"Stephan's right," Mei added. "We all need to do what we can or our planet and all the work, suffering, and sacrifice of everyone before us will be wasted."

John was not at all convinced and turned to Abir with a question. "What about all those Muslims killing each other and wantin' to kill us?"

"My people react to the hypocrisy and arrogance of those from the West in the only ways they know how. My people are as devout as yours, John, but are far poorer, far less educated, and have fewer opportunities. As my people become more educated, they will not..."

"Fly jets into our damn buildings as often?"

"Those people don't reflect the vast majority of Islam. Just like the man who blew up the building in Oklahoma City didn't reflect your values even though he claimed to be a Christian."

"David, what happens if we don't convince all seven billion people to change? Can't we just ignore the ones who won't cooperate and move on?" Stephan asked.

"We can't ignore them. They will cause chaos. If only 20,000 ISIS fighters can cause the damage they have, imagine what a few billion disgruntled folks with weapons can do. They will have to be dealt with if they don't cooperate."

"What does 'dealt with' mean?" Mei asked.

"In the end, I believe that once they hear their options, we will get cooperation from the followers of most major groups, including organized religions, countries, and the vast number of people on Earth. But if we don't, do you think it's fair that billions die and the history of Earth is wiped out because of one religion, or one rogue culture, or single country that refuses to cooperate?"

"You still haven't defined what you mean by 'dealt with'," Stephan said although he and the others already knew the answer.

"You know, dealt with. Gone. Dispatched. No more, you know... dealt with," David explained.

The group looked at David for the second time in fear.

David saw their reaction and responded, "You guys will have to determine what to do with a portion of the population on Earth that won't cooperate with anything you suggest. Some will opt for the Earth to simply disappear, like it never existed. All the art, all the music, all the scientific advancements, the heroism, all the tears, and all the hopes for future greatness and accomplishment, destroyed forever because some of the world's population will never, ever agree with any plan you come up with."

"So, should we just kill those who disagree with what we want to do?" Stephan asked.

"That's not my call, that's your call; it's your planet. But at some point, you have to put a value on the future existence of Earth and decide how high a price you want to pay for that future."

Not wanting to wade into that hot-button issue any further at that moment, Mei had a question. "David, are you the only one of your kind here on earth?"

"'My kind'? Hardly," David said with a small laugh.

"How many?"

"There's a lot of *my kind*. Always has been. Hey, we like your climate. We don't like the air pollution, or the traffic, and the TV programming sucks, but we can fix those things."

"How many, David? How many of you guys are here today?" Billy asked.

"Around two million, I guess."

"Two million!?" Billy said with a voice that had climbed two octaves.

"Give or take."

"What will all two million of you do when the rock smashes us all to hell?" Stephan asked.

"We'll start relocating our folks a few months in advance."

"Could any of us go with you?"

"Not a chance, Stephan. We've acclimatized over the centuries to Earth's atmosphere, pressure, and diseases. You guys couldn't survive on our planets, so coming with us isn't an option."

"So, as I understand it, we either change our world to what you and your Alliance think it should be, or we're all nuked like a colony of cockroaches. That about it?" Robert asked.

"That's a crude but an unfortunately accurate statement."

CHAPTER 21

AS DAVID SWEPT UP THE BROKEN glass with a small broom and dustpan, the group of seven sat silently around the table for several minutes pondering what he had said. They also considered their options, but there didn't appear to be any good ones.

"Guys, when I *knew* I was dying, I learned how important life was to me. Now that I've been given a second chance, I want to help the rest of the world get a second chance too. I say we do what we can in the next year and at least try to save this place," Stephan said.

"We'll need a helluva plan, and maybe a miracle or two," Robert said.

"If you guys form a plan, I'll help in the miracle department," David offered.

"You said you'd answer some questions for us, David. I know I have about a million," Robert said.

"I already answered a bunch including there's no God, at least as you define a god. Isn't that enough for one day?"

"Not when we have a ton more questions to ask," Billy said.

Okay, tell you what, I don't want to miss the Dodgers–Giants game this afternoon, so how about I give each of you a chance to ask one question? Anything at all and I'll do my best to answer them."

The group looked at each other wondering who would go first. "What happened at Roswell?" Stephan asked.

"It was a recon mission manned by outdated androids. They lost control of the ship and crashed the damn thing. No big deal. By the way, those androids are still in a cooler back at Wright-Patterson in Dayton. Let me know if you want to see them. I have some good friends working there."

Mei asked, "You said there were many of you already here, what do you call yourselves and…?"

"This won't be two questions, will it?"

"Okay, do your people living here know they are from another planet?" Mei clarified.

"Some do, some don't. Depends on if their parents decided to tell them. Also, not all of us are full blooded. For instance, a second generation couple could be half us and half you. Some could be 25 percent us, 75percent you or vice versa. It varies. But most of the world's population has at least a trace of our DNA."

"If you all don't believe in God, how come there ain't no crime where you live?" John asked.

"First of all, I live here on Earth, most of the time. But you really are hung up on that God thing, aren't you, John? First of all, your definition of a god is limited by your lack of knowledge of the universes that exists. The more advanced cultures are open to the idea that there is the possibility of a collective unconscious that is inherent in all sentient beings. It's something we all share. But in those cases, that collective unconscious is not defined in the form of a god or deity. Instead it's an internalized concept we all share, something no matter what we look like or where we come from. And I can tell you that there are some weird-looking folks out there, although they think we're funny looking too, but that's okay. As for the lack of crime? It's because where I come from, people don't hate each other like they do here. And why take something when everything is given to you for the asking?"

John did not respond to David's answer and instead stared into his glass of Diet Coke as if trying to understand the unthinkable.

After a few moments, Billy asked, "Does time travel exist?"

"Not exactly. But we do have something called "time penetration." It's pretty cool. Wanna see?"

David motioned for the group to follow him into the family room to the large screen HD TV on the wall. The group gathered around the back of his chair. David typed data into his computer. In seconds, a color image appeared.

It's the outside of a theater. Men are dressed in long black coats, and women wear silk gowns with ruffles. They carry umbrellas. The scene moves to the inside of a theater. The audience laughs at a comedy being performed on stage. Along the back of the theater, a lone man climbs several steps and makes his way to a door that he slowly opens.

He moves to the inside of the theater box that overlooks the stage twenty feet below. The handsome man aims a small pistol to the back of the head of a tall man in a black suit and fires one shot. Blood erupts from the tall man's eye and stains the dress of the small woman sitting next to him. She wails in anguish. The crowd in the theater shrieks. The picture on the TV freezes.

"My God, is that the Lincoln assassination? It looks real," Robert said.

"It is real. That's the real thing. You just saw Lincoln get shot in real time. I told you time penetration is pretty cool."

"But how in God's name...?" Robert tried to slide in another question.

"It would take quite a bit of time to explain. Besides, you'd need some classes in Time Sequencing and Advanced Event Recovery to understand the answer."

Robert fell back into a chair, astonished. "You mean you can revisit all historical events? From all time?"

"Not all of them. But we can retrieve a good number of them."

After several moments of digesting what they had seen, despite not really understanding it, the questions continued.

"What's the worst thing about Earth compared to other planets?" Billy asked.

"The designated hitter. Okay, okay just kidding, but that was a big fucking mistake by Bowie Kuhn. Worst thing about Earth? Earthlings. Slow to learn and adapt and, sorry to say, for the most part kind of worthless compared to what you see elsewhere. Nothing personal, but as a group you guys never quite made it to the finish line."

"We can't be too bad; you said you have lived here with us for over a 150 years," Billy said.

"It's the weather. You guys have really good weather. It's always seventy-two degrees and sunny somewhere. And your golf courses are terrific, too. Your sunsets are okay but can't compare with the purples, oranges, and greens on other places. Your food is so-so."

"How long do you intend to live, David?" Father Peña asked.

"I don't know. I still have a lot of work to do and that keeps me motivated. Guess I'll know when the time's right, but I figure another 400 to 500 years sounds reasonable. By the way, just so you know, even we wear out eventually, and things start to hurt."

Abir Ahmad was the last person to ask a question. He stared at David for several moments.

"You said you were born in 1873 and you look like you're forty. Do all your kind age the same way?"

"'Your kind'" again. That does sound a little racist, don't you think, Abir? But I won't hold it against you. Aging is something that's built into DNA. We found the aging gene, mutated it, and voilà, we live long lives. But we made sure you guys kept the old gene, you know, that population thing. Okay guys, that's it. Time for baseball. Tomorrow we begin to work on a plan."

David rose from his chair and moved to the kitchen where he grabbed two beers, a bag of nachos, some guacamole, salsa, and repaired to the den where he flipped on the TV and for the next three hours watched the Dodgers lose to the Giants 4–3 in extra innings.

While David watched baseball, the rest of the group dispersed. They walked up and down the ski slope, over creeks, into the woods. They tried to get their heads around everything David had told them over the previous twenty-four hours. They also began making mental notes for another round of questions.

CHAPTER 22

AFTER THE GROUP WANDERED AROUND the outside of David's house for several hours, one by one they eventually drifted back, ate a light dinner, and went to bed, with little more discussion among themselves. But none slept well. The numerous questions David had answered just led to other questions, which led to other questions, in a never-ending loop.

Over the next forty-eight hours the group, with David's input, began to formulate a plan. Their plan had several parts and was made up of short-term and long-term tactics and strategies that would include informing the world of David's existence and then the threat posed by Big Ben.

It was agreed that David's life would be in danger if he were to make any public appearances himself, or in any way identify himself, given the fact that many people on Earth had a nasty habit of preferring to shoot first and ask questions later. Especially when they are afraid, and it was agreed people would indeed be very afraid of what they would hear and may want to kill the messenger and/or David, or any of the group if they could.

Many of the discussions during the planning stage led to loud disagreements, accusations, door slamming, and even to vague and not so vague threats. Yet all seven hung in there. Even when they threatened to leave, something made them stop, return to their seats, and continue the hard slog of formulating a plan that would change—or end--the lives and/or future of every living thing on planet Earth.

After three full days of working, the group realized that what they had come up with was not a plan everyone agreed with or supported. Instead, it was a plan everyone hated. Maybe they hated it for different reasons, but they all hated it. They hated it because it ran counter to everything each of the seven stood for, believed in, and valued. But they knew something had to be done to protect Earth, and as many people on the planet that could be saved.

When the final document was prepared, agreed on, and signed by all, the group silently left the dining room table where the meeting had taken place and retired to their respective bedrooms to pack for their trip to New York City. It was comforting that they already knew they had flight plans to get them to Manhattan's Central Park with no security lines, baggage issues, or rude flight attendants…in seventeen minutes.

CHAPTER 23

TWO NIGHTS LATER, DAVID'S HANDPICKED group of seven waited patiently in a television network green room, nibbling on fresh fruit, crackers, M&M's and sipping bottled water and herbal tea. They had decided to execute the initial part of their plan of what lay in store for Earth by going on international TV to explain some of what David had told them.

There was one caveat for the initial public announcement. "I don't want no one bringin' up any of that 'no God' stuff," John had insisted. The rest of the group had agreed.

Long time FOX host Michael Evans, and self-described "voice for the poor and forgotten of America and the world," entered the green room to meet his guests for the night. He proudly displayed his $25,000 smile, $10,000 hairpiece, $2,000 suit, and $500 tie. "Evening folks and welcome. Okay, so I understand from my producer that you all met an alien and are going to tell your story here tonight, is that right?"

"That's all your producer told you? We met an alien?" Stephan asked.

"She said something about Roswell, an asteroid, and some religious stuff, but I really don't want to go 'religious' on this show. You know, that kind of thing can rile up people sometimes and hurt our ratings."

"Guys, this is going to be a waste of time, let's go," Robert said as he rose and headed to door. Evans stepped in front of Robert.

"Mr. President, please—you're the only reason we agreed to hear from this group. But aren't you afraid of risking your credibility and legacy by making some outrageous claims about men from outer space that can't be proven?"

"You know, Michael, you were always a fucking putz when I was in office, so I know you may be actually stupid enough to pass up the biggest story in the history of this planet. But believe me, we'll get our story out there with or without you. So either let us tell what we know the way we want to tell it, or get the hell out of our way," Robert said.

Evans looked at the other six who had also stood, ready to follow Robert, and simply nodded.

"Good evening, guests from around the world. Thank you for joining us from New York City. I'm your host, Michael Evans. Tonight we have a highly unusual show regarding a topic most of us have heard quite a bit about from newspapers, TV, and as reported by eyewitnesses. That being, the existence of aliens. Men from outer space. Since the supposed crash of an alien craft in Roswell, New Mexico, in 1947, our country has appeared to have a fixation about

*little green men, although no definitive proof has ever been produced
by any credible witnesses."*

After he introduced each of his guests, including their impressive
resumes, the group of seven sat around a large glass table, shook their heads,
and rolled their eyes listening to the "putz" continue his opening.

*"As I mentioned, among our guests tonight is former president Robert
Mitchell. Mr. President, welcome back to our program. Would you
please tell us how you got involved with this group and what this alien
stuff is all about?"*

*"When I was president, I had several briefings regarding what was
then called the UFO phenomenon. I saw detailed reports and even
photographic evidence that was difficult to ignore as to the existence of
UFOs and intelligent life from beyond this planet."*

*"But Mr. President, if this evidence was so compelling, why didn't you
or previous presidents release such information? Didn't you have an
obligation to American citizens and to the rest of the world to let us
know what you'd seen?"*

*"We had no hard evidence, and without definitive proof, as you just
called it, it was determined that such information could have created
a chaotic response from around the globe that could have jeopardized
world peace."*

*"Mr. President, with all due respect, are you really serious about all
this? I find it difficult to believe...*

*"Michael, I really don't give a damn what you believe or don't believe.
I'm here to tell your audience watching now from around the world the
truth of what has been proven to me and the rest of the folks you see
here tonight. After hearing what we have to say, you and your audience
can decide if you choose to believe our message or not."*

*Turning to his right, Evans asked, "Dr. Mei Liu, you are a professor
of physics at MIT and highly respected in your field of astrophysics.
Do you concur with President Mitchell?"*

*"I agree with everything President Mitchell said and will add that in
addition to what we will explain tonight, we are prepared to provide
some physical demonstrations of the existence and the power of a
significant alien presence on this planet."*

*"Oh, are they going to stop all the cars in the world like in The Day
the Earth Stood Still?* Evans asked with a laugh as he looked

into the camera and displayed really nice teeth.

"They could, but that would be disruptive and maybe even dangerous. This will be more fun. Rather than disabling cars around the world, how about we take you off the air around the world for thirty seconds?" Mei asked.

"And how do you intend...?"

The FOX director in the control room began to freak out into his headset. "What the fuck is going on?! We just went dark. Camera two, are you still on?! Jesus H. Christ what the fuck...?"

Mei and the rest of the group sat quietly and smiled as Michael Evans listened to chaos through his earpiece. "What do you mean we're off the air?"

Billy gave a thumbs-up to Mei, who smiled.

"Doctor Liu, it appears you have interfered with our broadcast, which is a federal crime punishable by..."

In his earpiece, Evans heard the good news. "Okay, Michael, we're back...everybody grab your seats...Michael...go!"

"Dr. Liu, we apparently lost our broadcast signal for a period of time and..."

"It was just for thirty seconds to get your attention. Let's go for sixty this time to let you know we are serious."

"Dammit, we're dark again," the director yelled into Evan's earpiece. "No audio or video. What the fuck is that bitch doing?"

Billy sat between Mei and Stephan and high-fived both of them at FOX's broadcast angst.

"Dr. Liu, we're calling security and you're going to get your ass thrown in jail for what you are doing to a live international broadcast. This is outrageous!"

"Michael, when we are back on the air, I suggest you listen to what we have to say and stop being such a condescending asshole, or you'll be off the air for a week," Robert said.

"Okay, we're back for now," the director said. "Go, Michael, and let that bitch say what she wants."

"Dr. Liu, it will be difficult for you to present your message to our viewers around the world if we are not on the air..."

"We could always go over to CNN, MSNBC, or CBS. I bet they

would listen to us now."

"Listen to what, Dr. Liu?" an exasperated Evans asked.

"Several weeks ago, all of us around this table were invited to attend a meeting in Colorado. That meeting has changed all our lives. We found out things no human has ever learned before," Mei said.

"From an alien?"

"From someone who looks exactly like us but comes from another planet," Robert said.

"Which planet?"

"The name is irrelevant, but the message he gave us is vitally important to everyone on Earth," Billy interjected.

"What is the message or is that irrelevant too?" Evans asked.

"It is a message that has now been confirmed by physicists all over the world. In less than a year, Earth will be struck by an asteroid so large it will destroy every living thing on this planet," Robert said.

"Mr. President, that is a reckless and unconfirmed theory that many eminent scientists around the world disagree with..."

"Are those the same scientists who said there is no global warming? The so-called scientists of whom you speak were dead wrong then and are dead wrong now. A new study confirming the strike will be released tomorrow morning, and it will also confirm the existence of the asteroid and the subsequent annihilation it will cause on this planet," Mei said.

"Your alien friend told you this was going to occur?"

"Yes. He also told us he and those from his planet could prevent such an occurrence but we, as a unified global civilization, must meet certain conditions," Mei said.

"What does he want? Our women, our gold, our..."

"Listen you condescending smart-ass...this fucking planet is in deep shit, and dicks like you are part of the problem," Stephan virtually spat.

Stephan looked away from Evans, then directly into camera and continued.

"We want everyone around the world to clearly hear and to understand exactly what we are saying. Over the next several months, we will be traveling around the world explaining our options with regard to saving our planet. Very simply, we can make changes, or we can, and will, perish. All of us. Those of you who wish to join a new world order unshackled by governments, boundaries, religious orders, prejudices, and stupidity will find billions of others who will share your hopes and dreams. Those of you who persist in living in a past filled with lies, superstition, narrow-mindedness, poverty, and sickness, will have no future. No future at all. Neither will the planet Earth."

"That sounds like a threat, Stephan," Michael said.

"Forgive me for being vague. It is a threat, a definitive, unambiguous, crystal clear threat. But it should also sound like an opportunity, Michael. And unlike you, I hope the people watching this program will be smart enough to take advantage of such an opportunity. Because if they are not smart enough to do so, life on this planet will cease to exist," Stephan said.

For several moments, silence pervaded the FOX set. Then the group of seven got up and walked off the newsroom set, leaving Evans alone. And speechless.

"Okay, Michael, we've had enough dead air tonight...go," his director said.

Evans turned to the camera. *"Ladies and gentlemen, we just had the most remarkable interview I've ever been involved with in my thirty-year career. A group of highly respected professionals from various walks of life are saying that aliens exist. They claim they actually met one. They also claim an asteroid is headed to Earth, and the only way we will be saved is to acquiesce to changing the way we live our lives on our own planet."*

The group of seven stopped in the lobby after leaving the studio and watched Michael Evans wrap up his show. *"For everyone at FOX, I want to personally apologize to each of you for what I will only call the bane of live television. We not only had technical difficulties tonight, including losing our seven-second delay, which led to some things to come over the air that were not only profane and ridiculous, but we also heard things that were dangerous and irresponsible. I know this audience is too intelligent to believe what our guests were presenting this evening and furthermore...*

65

Mei shook her head and said, "Wow, that guy is a putz."

In the FOX control room, the director screamed, "Fuck me! We're dead again!! Goddamn it all to hell!"

"How long this time, Mei?" Billy asked.

"I like Chris Wallace on Sunday morning. That's only three days off."

The group of seven exited the FOX building and found a place that served outstanding deep-dish pizza.

CHAPTER 24

OVER THE NEXT TWENTY-FOUR hours, there was enormous worldwide reaction to the controversial FOX broadcast. Much of it was violent. There were endless TV and internet images of riots from every corner of the world, including Vatican Square, which was crowded with millions of people praying. Times Square was filled with millions more carrying signs regarding the end of the world. The Wailing Wall in Jerusalem was packed and overwhelmed with worshipers. Churches, synagogues, and mosques were filled to capacity with the faithful and fearful.

World leaders, including the Pope, spoke to their legions of followers and tried to calm fears, but nothing seemed to work. The UN was called into emergency session, but delegates yelled and screamed at each other, and as a result, no one heard anyone. The same happened in the U.S. Congress., in Parliament, and in every other governmental body from small towns to world powers. The world collectively yelled and screamed. But no one listened.

In the White House, current president Thomas McKay was in Cabinet meeting when he was told that former president Robert Mitchell was on the phone, returning the president's call. McKay put Mitchell on speakerphone so everyone could hear the conversation.

"Bob, what the fuck were you thinking last night going on FOX like that?"

"My dear Mr. President, so good to hear from you."

"God dammit, Bob, we have messes on our hands in New York, LA, Miami, and Chicago. NATO called and all hell's breaking loose in London, Paris, Rome, Tehran, and all over the damn place because of you and those loonies you hang with. The stock market has fallen over 5000 points and we had to go to DEFCON 1 this morning. The Joint Chiefs think this is a Russian plot and want me to start bombing Moscow within the hour."

"So, Tom, you don't believe anything you heard last night?"

"Bob, I've read the same reports on UFOs you did, but putting that stuff on worldwide TV was fucking stupid. You should know better than that. That was irresponsible and dangerous."

"Tom, every word we said last night is true. The alien part is really the secondary story here. An asteroid is going to blow Earth all to hell in eleven months if we don't agree to the terms our alien contact has presented to us."

"Terms? You mean all that stuff I read today about churches going away, removal of boundaries between countries, eliminating use of fossil fuels, and all that other crap? You know damn well that stuff wouldn't be enforceable even if we said it was the law."

"I know it won't be easy, but it really is the only chance for Earth to survive. These guys are serious. They believe we're killing the planet anyway, and they won't lift a finger to save it or us if we don't agree to change how we manage our planet."

"They sound like a bunch of damn tree huggers."

"It's way more than that, Tom. They want us to stop killing each other in ridiculous wars fueled mainly by religious zealotry and arbitrary boundaries. They want us to become a truly human race, not a race among nations for dominance, power, and wealth."

"My God, Bob, you sound like you have lost your damn mind."

"Tom, everyone knows I am smarter than you. Even you. But I hope you are at least smart enough to listen to and understand that what we are saying is true. If you don't listen and don't begin to take immediate steps to do what needs to be done, this planet and everyone on it is history. You must understand that a year from today, none of us will be here, and this planet will be a piece of charcoal if you and the rest of the world leaders don't act."

"What the hell as we supposed to do, close all the churches, ignore boundaries, and eliminate fossil fuels? The worldwide economy would crash overnight; the rioting we are seeing now would get a hundred times worse."

"Then let it get a hundred times worse, and maybe people will finally listen to what we are saying."

"What do you mean, let the entire world go hell because some guy convinced you and your idiot friends that a rock is going to maybe hit Earth?"

"Tom, it will hit the Earth, and there is nothing anyone can do about it— that fact has been confirmed by every scientist in the world. The Earth will not be damaged; it will be annihilated, utterly destroyed, and the only way we avoid that is to agree to the conditions set by the man we are talking to."

"You actually believe these guys have the power to do what they say? I mean, could they really destroy the asteroid even if they got what they wanted?"

"Starting at noon today, they're going to give three demonstrations of their power in three different parts of the world that they say will prove their capability. You can watch it on TV, except for FOX."

CHAPTER 25

IN NEW YORK CITY, A TV reporter from a local station stood a block away from an old ten-story office building on 84th Street that was in the process of being torn down. Cameras from all the networks focused on the young female reporter with the building seen in the distance over her right shoulder.

> *"This morning, the media was notified that the first of three demonstrations of the alien's power will be put on display at this abandoned building. The event is said to commence and end at exactly 12 noon. We have no idea how just blowing up or somehow destroying a building will demonstrate unusual power but we will soon see. We were told there is no danger for spectators but as you can see, we are keeping our distance."*

The TV cameras moved to the building. In the background a church bell rang eleven times. On the twelfth ring, a light beam from the sky hit the building, and it completely disappeared in less than a second. No explosion. No sound. No fire. No smoke. No remains of the building. It was simply and utterly gone.

> *"Oh my God! I'm not sure what just happened, but an entire building has simply vanished!"* The reporter said. *"Charles Becker, PhD. and professor of physics at Columbia University, is with us today to analyze what just occurred. Sir, what did you see and is it a significant display of power?"*

As she spoke, the reporter and a speechless Dr. Becker walked toward what had become a vacant lot.

> *"An entire building has been vaporized in less than a second. What kind of weapon could do that?"* the reporter asked.

Professor Becker still didn't answer. After they reached the lot, the professor poked the ground with a detector of some kind.

> *"Was it a nuclear weapon?"* the reporter asked.

> *"No, there is no sign of any radiation."* Professor Becker said softly.

> *"Then what could cause this building to…?"*

> *"You don't understand, there's no evidence of this building. Even the basement*

has been...it's just gone." Becker said with awe in his voice.

"What kind of power does this signify?"

"We will have to do some chemical analysis of the remaining soil, but it appears whatever ray hit this building is capable of destroying matter."

"But matter is something that cannot be destroyed, at least that is what I thought."

"Destroying matter is indeed not possible, at least based on our knowledge of physics, but it appears that is what has occurred."

"Dr. Becker, do you believe what we saw on TV last night and what you just witnessed indicates an alien presence on Earth?"

"Well, all I can say is, whatever or whoever vaporized this building possesses a power we do not."

Exactly one hour later in Egypt, an Al Jazeera reporter stood in front of the Great Pyramid at Giza. The reporter appeared nervous and concerned. *"Based on what we saw an hour ago in New York City, where a building was vaporized in a second, Egyptian citizens and officials are frantic that the Great Pyramid here at Giza is at risk of being destroyed. It was learned earlier today that this would be the location of the alien's second display of power one hour after the New York demonstration."*

The reporter stood out of way and the camera focused on the Pyramid. Without warning, a silent ray descended from the sky and enveloped the pyramid. Seconds later the pyramid rose twenty feet into the air and turned 180 degrees. It was bathed in a blinding blue-white light. Within seconds more, it was returned to its original position but was now clad in glistening marble including a solid gold triangular cap at the peak of the structure, exactly how it was constructed in 2560 BC.

"Praise be to Allah!! The pyramid has been...transformed!! Before our very eyes! It is beautiful beyond words! What power could create such magnificence!?" the reported gasped.

Inside the Sandy Knoll Retirement Home in Biloxi, Mississippi, a half dozen local reporters waited in a hallway after being alerted that the third and final display of power would take place in the room of Dixie Smith, a 102-year-old woman who suffered from dementia and assorted other ailments. She had been unresponsive for nearly a year. At precisely 2:00 p.m. her doctor entered her room and injected her IV with contents from a vial of liquid. He turned and faced the one camera allowed in the small room.

"This morning we received a call stating that with the permission of Miss Smith's only living relative, we were to inject her with what was delivered to this hospital and described as a "cure" for Miss Smith's ailments. I informed the caller and her relative that Miss Smith was not sick but just old. Very, very old."

As the doctor spoke, the cameraman and those in the hallway peered into the room and began to gasp and appear to be in shock. The camera moved in for a close-up of Dixie's face and upper body on the bed. They saw a transformation. She began to get younger. Her wrinkles slowly melted away, replaced with fresh pink skin, her thin gray hair returned to a thick golden blonde, her age spots dissolved, her breasts became firm, her teeth returned. Over a twelve-minute period, she morphed into an attractive woman of twenty-two years old.

In stunned silence the doctor moved to her side and looked at her pulse and blood pressure readings on the machine next to her bed. He ran his hands down her arms, lifted her eyelids, and shone a light into her eyes. When he did, Dixie woke up, looked around the room and asked, "Am I in heaven?"

"No, this is Biloxi." The doctor answered.

"Okay then, Well, I think I'm ready to go home now." Dixie said.

The doctor nodded numbly and mumbled something unintelligible, right before he picked up the vial from the table and tried to suck out the remaining liquid.

CHAPTER 26

IN A SUITE AT THE Sofitel Hotel on West 44th Street in Manhattan, the group of seven sat in front of the TV and gaped at Dixie Smith being interviewed by reporters. She seemed a bit confused by what had happened to her, and kept looking into the mirror someone had given to her. "Are you sure I'm not dead and in heaven?" she asked several times.

"Incredible," Robert said.

"I guess David did provide the miracle part. Do you think the world believes us now?" Stephan asked.

"I'm not even sure I believe it," Billy said.

Mei's cell phone rang. It was David, Mei put him on speakerphone.

"So, how'd I do, guys? Too much? Not enough?" David asked.

"I'd say you certainly got people's attention," Robert said.

"There will of course be many who will say that everything they saw today was faked, like a movie with CGI. But there will be many others who will believe what they saw and want to join us," Abir said.

"David, we need to call ourselves and this movement something. I was thinking of the United Peoples of Earth. What do you think?" Stephan asked.

"Call yourselves Hootie and the Blowfish for all I care, we just need to convince my folks that, like Sam Cooke said, "a change is gonna come.""

"Such calls for change will initially create more unrest and violence than exists even now. Are your people patient?" Abir asked.

"Only if they see progress. But they're really hung up on the population thing. They know that is the main reason the Earth is dying. Too many people and too few resources. You guys need to work on that issue ASAP."

"How do we *work* on such a thing? The population is what it is," Father Peña said.

"That's up to you guys to figure out, but I'm just telling you it's a dealbreaker."

"There are over seven billion people on the planet today. What population number are you guys looking at?" Robert asked.

"Less," David said flatly.

CHAPTER 27

AFTER DAVID'S CALL, THE GROUP of seven sat around the suite and discussed options regarding population. "How about we get every country to agree to population control like they already have in China?" Mei asked.

"That would take decades to effect change, " Father Peña said. "I think the Alliance is looking for something much more immediate."

"In a bizarre way, David was right when he said the Earth needs illnesses, plagues, wars, and all that stuff to help control population," Billy offered. "It's cruel to say it, but significantly reducing the population would create a better life for the survivors."

"Sounds like a good plan if you and your family are on the list of survivors. Not so good if you're not on the list," Robert said.

"It's simple math. To reduce population, we need more people dying than being born. Based on what David said, the death rate must go up substantially," Abir said.

"Well, we sure as hell can't go 'round killin' a bunch of folks just to satisfy David and his posse," John stated with finality.

The group looked at each other for over a minute; an uncomfortable silence pervaded the room. Finally, Billy said, "That may be exactly what we have to do to save the planet."

"Are you crazy, man? You mean your idea of population control is murder, extermination? You sound like a damn Nazi motherfucker," John shouted.

"Ever hear of culling the herd? It's what farmers do when they run out of food to feed the whole flock. They kill some, so others can live," Billy said.

"Look, we all know that's not something we'd really ever consider doing, but let's look at it as an intellectual exercise," Robert suggested.

"Well, first, you'd need a number, a target of some kind. What would David and his group feel the magic number is in terms of population reduction? Is it a 100,000 people? A million? Four million?" Stephan asked.

"This is crazy talk," John said disgustedly.

"Given what we saw this morning at that building that totally disappeared, body disposal would not be an issue. That would eliminate disease," Mei said.

"Let's say it's a million people. Just for the sake of discussion, how would you select who would die? Who would live?" Stephan asked.

"Like the farmer culling his head, we'd start with the old and sick. I mean, why save an old cow?" Billy asked.

"It would have to be more than age alone. Some older people can be far more productive than younger people. Or how about a sick young person compared to a healthy older person? What then?" Robert asked.

"Sounds like you're protecting the senior citizen class, Robert," Stephan said.

"No, I'm not, it's just that…"

"What if it was done on cultural or nationality basis?" Father Peña suggested.

"You mean like erasing an entire country, José?" Robert asked.

"A country may not be enough. How about an entire continent?" Billy suggested.

"I think you'd want to see an even across-the-board reduction around the world. More random. That's the fairest way," Mei offered.

"Are you listening to yourselves? You're talking about mass murder! Killin' innocent folks," John said.

"John, would you put a gun to the head of a single random person and pull the trigger to save hundreds?" Robert asked.

"That ain't what you're all sayin. You're talkin' about killin' millions, hell, billions of innocent people. I say we all die together. It's not fair to pick some to live and some to die. You all are tryin' to play God. It just ain't right," John said.

"No John, it is very right. Nations do that all the time. I did it when I was president. You send x-number of people into war knowing that some will, without question, die. Their certain deaths, even though statistically a small percentage, are considered acceptable loses, and will save millions of lives. All nations have done it for all of recorded history. Some die to protect a country, an idea, or a religion. It's no different here. But again…we are just theorizing—we wouldn't really…"

"Who are we kidding, Robert?" Stephan asked. "If we believe David, and I think we all do, we have to do something drastic to save this planet and come up with a plan to…"

"To what…murder a billion damn people?" The rest of the group was quiet and stared at John.

"John, I don't think a billion will be near enough for David and his buddies," Billy said.

The group became quiet again and watched as violent riots from all corners of the world were shown endlessly on every TV station.

CHAPTER 28

LATER THAT NIGHT IN HER hotel room, Mei spoke with David on her cell phone. "David, I just left the others, and it's not going well here. The population issue is now front and center, and the idea of killing an untold number of innocent people is something everyone is against."

"I knew it would be, but it's a nonstarter with my people. They will need to see a plan that addresses that fundamental problem, or they won't help."

"Even if we somehow can deal with the population issue, and that seems impossible at this point, the religion and borders issues are just as problematic. There is simply no agreement among the seven of us on how we move forward."

"I assumed that was the case. I think we need to meet ASAP, and we can discuss the issues. I may have some ideas that will help you and your group. I can pick you up in Central Park in twenty minutes."

"Where are you now?" Mei asked.

"Miami."

In less an hour, Mei was having a Mai Tai on David's 110' Feadship docked in Biscayne Bay. After getting a tour of the yacht, Mei noted, "You certainly live well for a..."

"Just call me a foreigner. You know, sort of like you." David said.

"What job do you have to afford a ship like this?"

"The stock market is a wonderful thing, especially when you can help certain folks build businesses in the technology sector by giving them little hints on how things work. I guess it could be called the ultimate insider trading."

Mei changed subjects. "Why did you want to see me tonight?"

"I was worried about how your meetings were going and wanted to know how I could help."

"Answer me this—how many people have to die to placate your Alliance?"

"That's your decision."

"You mean we just start killing people until you say 'enough.' That's insane, David, and you know it."

"Reducing population is not for the benefit of the Alliance. It's for the benefit of those who would remain on this planet and the planet itself. You can decide to do nothing, and everyone will die in less than a year. But even if there was no asteroid, this planet is dead. Can't you see that?" David asked.

"It's incredible to me that I'm part of a group even remotely contemplating killing billions of our citizens."

"There's a viable option. Do nothing. Truly, that is an option you shouldn't discount, Mei. There is a certain symmetry in everyone on the planet dying at once. As if a story ends with no sequel possible."

"We have seriously discussed that option, and I think Reverend John and Father Peña would be okay with that choice."

"What about the rest of you?"

"No one is for killing anyone, but the option of the entire planet dying is utterly unacceptable to most of us. But even if we were to agree to go forward with..."

"A reduction?"

"If we're to go forward, we have no idea what kinds of numbers you guys are looking for or how we would...you know."

"If you make the decision to move ahead, I can provide equipment and train you on what methods and tools will work."

"This is unbelievable... the whole thing. Our world, all the people in it, all the history, all the art, all the suffering to bring us to this point it's…" Mei began to sob. David moved next to her on the couch and put his arm around her shoulder.

"Mei, there's another option. I can give you something that will make you forget all this, and you can let the others carry out the plan. You won't remember anything including me. Your life can go on as before."

"Passing that kind of responsibility to someone else doesn't solve the problem."

"No group on this planet has ever had a more difficult decision to make," David said.

Mei pulled away from David and wiped her tears from her eyes. "One last question. What guarantees do we have that if we do what's needed, your friends will destroy the asteroid?"

"Sorry to say, there are no guarantees. But there'd be no reason to let the planet be destroyed if it had a chance for survival by the actions you'd take. Any group responsible enough to do what has to be done now would be the kinds of stewards of Earth that would do the right things in the future."

"We can't take that chance. You guys need to destroy the asteroid first before we would even consider killing billions of our own people."

"The Alliance would never agree to such a deal. If we destroyed the asteroid first, I would assume your group would not live up to our agreement and do what needed to be done. You would simply refuse to carry out your end of the bargain. I think you know I'm right about that."

"Then is it possible that we could do it simultaneously?" Mei asked.

David got up and walked around the salon of the ship, mulling over Mei's suggestion. After several moments, he said, "That would be tricky, but I guess it might be possible. Let me think about how we could work out those details."

Mei looked out of the yacht's windows onto shimmering Biscayne Bay lit up by the Miami skyline. "I need to get back to Boston. We decided we'd work there in a conference room at MIT starting tomorrow afternoon."

"Okay but you have to eat something. How about dinner at Joe's and I'll have you back in Boston twenty minutes later?"

CHAPTER 29

AT JOE'S STONE CRAB, MEI and David sat at an outside table next to the water that lapped gently against a concrete foundation on which the restaurant was constructed. A gentle breeze blew in from the southwest across the water bringing with it the salty fishy smell of ocean.

After some idle conversation, they ordered a bottle of white wine and dinner. When both arrived, David wasted no time digging into an order of King Crab legs, rice, and a salad. Mei just picked at her crab cake dinner between sips of wine.

"You need to eat, rest, and take care of yourself, Mei. If you and the team wear down, it helps no one," David said as he dipped a forkful of crab leg into melted butter.

"I know, but it's hard to eat, drink, or sleep, and not think about what needs to be done."

"Just think of the alternative."

"I do. Believe me, I do."

"Hey, you a baseball fan?"

Caught off guard by the change in topics, Mei answered, "I guess... even though the Red Sox have sucked the last few years."

"How about we take in the Yanks-Sox tomorrow night at Fenway?"

"I couldn't go to a baseball game...not now."

"You need to relax and..."

"I won't be able to relax. Not when I may have to help kill..."

"I understand, but think of all of those you'll save, Mei."

After trying but failing to get Mei to finish her dinner and join him in trying some of Joe's famous key lime pie, they finally headed back to David's yacht in a dinghy after dinner. When they reached the back of yacht, David helped Mei up out of the small boat onto the deck of the Feadship. As he pulled her up, he brought her close to him, wrapped his arms around her, and kissed her. She pulled away at first, but he continued to hold her around the waist. She looked into his eyes then passionately kissed him back.

David picked up Mei and carried her to his bedroom and laid her on his bed. A dim overhead light shone down on Mei. Her eyes were shut. Her face had an expression of calm. Her breathing was steady. She heard soft music in the background and felt herself drift to a place of serenity she had not felt before.

After staring down at her for several minutes, David unbuttoned Mei's dress and unsnapped her front-clasped bra. Her eyes remained closed as he kissed her neck before he moved his mouth to her breasts. She continued to drift on a wave of pleasure knowing she shouldn't be enjoying what was happening to her, but she was powerless to stop it. *Why stop it now,* she concluded, *after all in a year…*

David stood up and took off his shirt and slacks. He was tan, lithe, and muscular. He removed Mei's dress. He kissed her flat stomach then moved his head down below her waist, Mei moaned and felt the almost imperceptible movement of the huge yacht beneath her. She could feel David's warm breath on her body. She felt the wetness of his mouth. She gave up trying to fight her inner battle of conscience. *The hell with it,* she thought.

CHAPTER 30

THE NEXT MORNING DAVID LAY on his left side, his back facing Mei. He snored slightly. Mei's eyes opened slowly. They closed and then opened wide again as she figured out where she was and who was next to her. She bolted up in bed, looked around and gasped. She gaped at David who remained asleep. Mei saw her clothes on the floor in a pile next to David's.

"Oh, my God," Mei whispered.

David rolled over on his back, stretched, yawned, opened his eyes, and saw Mei. "Morning, sunshine," he said with a smile.

"What the hell happened last night?"

David smiled and reached for Mei. "Better to show than tell."

Mei angrily pulled away from David. "I mean it, what happened last night? I don't remember anything...tell me what happened."

"First of all, I was absolutely terrific and..."

"Did you drug me?"

"Drug you? Are you insane? You were awake the whole time and unless you fake it better than anyone I've ever been with, you had about four "crashers." You even woke me at three this morning for an encore."

"I don't believe you. Answer me—did you put something in my drink?"

"No, Mei, I didn't put something in your drink or food or anything else. Believe me, everything you did was of your own free will."

"I would not have slept with you...not this soon...not..."

"Really? Want to see a tape replay?"

"What!?"

"When you saw my video camera on the desk last night, you asked me to tape everything so we could remember our 'first time.' You said that it would be romantic. Here, look."

David took the remote and clicked on the TV. A replay of the previous night's activity began with Mei lying naked on the king-size bed looking into the camera smiling and waving then asking. "You promise you won't show this to anybody, will you?"

On the tape, David said, "No, of course not, like you said it's just keeping a memory for us. You know, the first time."

"I've never done this before," Mei could be seen saying with a slight giggle.

"Wow, you are beautiful," David had responded.

The TV screen showed scenes of David and Mei making love. Mei was very wide awake and apparently enjoying herself and even looked directly into the camera several times during the event. David clicked off the tape. Mei lay in bed and stared at the blank TV screen in shock.

"I don't remember...any of it. I can't believe I did such a thing. I am so embarrassed."

"Hey, you're under a lot of stress and we did kill two bottles of wine at Joe's and had a couple drinks here. But I'd never take advantage of you...I thought you were enjoying yourself."

"I need to go back to Boston, now."

David touched Mei's shoulder. "I was under the impression you at least liked me, especially after..."

"David, I do like you, but I don't understand what happened last night. That's not me. That's not something I would do, at least not the first time..."

"Hey, I could say I'll just forget last night but I can't. I've been attracted to you since Aspen. I can't really help that."

"Can your little toy take me to Boston?"

"Sure...let me grab a shower. In fact we could save water, if we..."

"You shower first...alone."

"There you go wasting a natural resource," David smiled at Mei, who gave him a half- smile back.

On the ride back to Boston David asked, "When can I see you again?"

"David, I'm in no emotional state to see anyone. Not with what we have to do."

"You need someone in your life now more than ever. I know what you're going through. I can help."

"I don't know...I need some time to think."

"Look, I'm never more than twenty minutes away from anywhere in the world. If you need company, anytime, anywhere, just call."

David's craft landed unseen in a small park adjacent to MIT. Mei exited the craft and walked toward the physics building a hundred yards away. A puzzled student on a bike saw Mei walk from the park as if she had appeared from nowhere. As he stared at Mei, his bike hit the curb and he fell over, dropping his physics and calculus textbook and notes all over the sidewalk.

As she walked past the young man, Mei helped him pick up his books and papers and said, "I hope you're not drinking and riding. That can be dangerous."

"No, I didn't...I...just...I mean... I thought...where did you...?

Mei smiled at the young man and walked toward her office.

CHAPTER 31

IN A CONFERENCE ROOM INSIDE the MIT physics department, the group of seven sat around a large table littered with books, water bottles, maps, laptop computers, coffee cups, and plates of uneaten and dried-out food.

"What about engaging the governments of the world in these decisions?" Abir asked.

"No government would ever agree to kill its own citizens, even if it meant saving Earth," Robert said.

"Mei, did David give you a magic number?" Billy asked.

"All he said was we have more than twice as many people on Earth than it can currently support."

"That's three and a half billion people," Robert noted.

"Look, I've been thinking about this and the fact is, all seven billion people on this planet are already dead. They just don't know it yet," Stephan said.

"I agree. We wouldn't be killing billions; we'd be saving billions," Billy offered.

"That's what David told me last night."

"But how would we actually—I mean that's a lot of people..." Billy said.

"David would show us how to use the technology he used on the building in New York. He said it would be instantaneous and painless," Mei offered.

A silence fell over the conference room. John sat at the end of table and shook his head.

"Folks, there is no way on God's green earth, no way, I can be part of this plan for mass murder."

Mei turned to John and said, "John, I can completely understand how you feel, and I think all of us have had those same thoughts. We do truly have an option we should all consider. We can do nothing, and everyone on Earth dies and the planet becomes uninhabitable for thousands of years. Every single living thing would be dead. I'm very serious; that is truly a viable option. Or we can make incredibly horrific decisions and save half the people in the world and our planet."

"In reality, do we really have a choice? I don't think so. What we do have is a terrible obligation that none of us asked for. John, do you believe what's written in the Bible?" Robert asked

"I surely do, every word."

"Then how is what we are contemplating any different than what

God did with the flood? He killed everyone on Earth except for Noah and his family and what they saved on the ark."

"None of us is God. None of us has the right to decide to kill our brothers and sisters. It just ain't right, and nothing y'all say is gonna make me feel any different."

Mei looked at John for several moments and said, "John, it's hardly a decision or a choice. What Robert said is true. What has been thrust upon us is in fact a terrible obligation. An obligation and decision that no one in the history of the world has ever had to make before. By doing what has to be done, we can save half the world's population and the planet itself. But doing so will require us to make horrendous decisions. Very simply we have to ask ourselves, is it better to save half the world or lose it all?"

John did not respond to Mei. Instead, he buried his head in his hands and stared down at the floor.

"Death on such an incredible scale will require massive killings. How could such events even be carried out?" Abir asked.

"David said the events could be simultaneous; in fact, I insisted on that provision. We'd make our selections, then input the geographic coordinates. We would then direct a series of rays with a computer that would be launched at exactly the same time the Alliance destroys the asteroid. He said the rays are 100% effective and accurate down to a millimeter."

"Did your insistence on simultaneous events stem from not trusting David?" Stephan asked.

"When you are dealing with billions of lives, I would trust no one," Mei said.

Robert asked, "How do we avoid the destruction of trillions of dollars of infrastructure?"

"David explained that we can't avoid all destruction, but we'd reduce it significantly by bringing people together in large groups in areas out in the open."

"We could always sponsor a free Justin Bieber outdoor concert. People would welcome death after that," Billy said. The comment broke the tension in the room, and everyone laughed. Except John.

"What would really draw people outside in such mass numbers all at the same time?" José asked.

"How about the Pope?" Billy asked.

"He would never knowingly agree to such a plan," José said.

"How about a really, really big fucking explosion?" Billy proffered.

The group looked at each other for several moments.

"The destruction of the asteroid?" Mei asked.

"Hell yes. I'd sure as hell go outside to see that thing zapped," Billy said.

"It would be like when people go outside to see an eclipse," Robert said.

"Or a witch burning," Billy offered.

"The press could promote the destruction of the asteroid in advance, let people know where it could best be seen around the world. People could be directed to open areas like deserts, fields, even the polar regions, away from cities and structures," Mei suggested.

"What if nobody shows up?" José asked.

"Then we'd have to focus on large urban areas like Shanghai, Mumbai, Delhi, Istanbul and..."

"How about New York, Chicago, LA?" Abir asked.

At end of the table, Billy tapped away on his laptop. "It wouldn't be enough."

"What do you mean, not enough?" Abir asked.

"If every single person in the ten largest cities in the world was eliminated, that's only a hundred and thirty million people, roughly four percent of what we'd need."

"Four percent? Dear God," José said.

"In addition to massing people in certain locations, we need to think in terms of countries. Big fuckers like India, Indonesia, Pakistan, Bangladesh...," Billy said.

"You have conveniently overlooked the US as a source for elimination," Abir noted.

"I didn't overlook it. I simply made a value judgement that three hundred million relatively educated, healthy, and organized Americans would be a better bet for the world in the future than the same amount of uneducated, AIDS-ridden, unorganized people living in nineteenth-century countries like in West Africa," Billy said flatly.

"What a condescendingly asinine statement... but typical of the American view of the world."

"Okay, Abir, how about this...we zap all of China and India, then throw in the entire African continent. That gets us to our 3.5 billion goal." Billy said as he snapped his fingers for emphasis.

"Who said that's our goal? We're guessing. Further, it appears your list would essentially wipe out most of the Islamic religion."

"Okay, you keep Iraq, and Iran and...," Billy countered.

"For God's sake, this ain't fantasy football or some damn video game. Are you seriously thinking of wiping out most of Asia and Africa?" John asked.

"We have to consider what happens to the remaining world economies if populations of entire countries or continents were eliminated," Robert said.

Stephan agreed. "Robert's right. China makes a lot of shit for the rest of the world now. That stuff would also be needed later."

"I think an evenhanded approach is best. We take an equal percent from each city and country," José said.

"That's bullshit. You really think there should be no weight given to what a certain country or group of people can contribute to the planet in terms of brain power, production, or other assets?" Billy asked.

"What about their use of natural resources? Americans have the largest carbon footprint in the world. Eliminating half their population would be a boon to humanity," Abir accurately noted.

"What about the Middle East? Take those folks off the planet, and we have no wars, plenty of oil, and no damn terrorists," John offered.

"You including Israel in that group?"

"Israel ain't bombing buildings and flyin' jets into buildings and..."

"No, they bomb our mosques killing our women and children. They assassinate scientists and steal our holy land."

Tired of the arguments, Mei got up from the table, walked to the window, and saw a blue cloudless sky. A perfect Boston day. At that moment, she knew what needed to be done. She interrupted the growing debate behind her and said, "Gentlemen, in just a few minutes, our prejudices, biases, and preconceived concepts of the world have become obvious. This is not a decision that can or should be made by a committee. It should be made by one person."

"Who?" Abir asked.

"Me."

"Why you, Mei?"

"I've lived all over the world. The fact is I have no true allegiance to a country, religion, culture, or political agenda. All those things have always seemed foolish and infantile to me, almost tribal."

"After hearing all this the last few days, I have to agree it must be a single person," Robert said. "But Mei, do you realize the enormity of what you're putting on your shoulders? There has never been a decision like this in the history of the world."

"I know what's at stake. But absent agreement that everyone on earth should die, this decision must be made. And no group could ever come to a consensus over such an issue. We proved that today."

The rest of group sat in silence and looked at Mei for several minutes. Finally, Billy and Stephan simultaneously closed their laptops. Robert closed the two large books in front of him. Others slowly gathered their belongings.

"I agree that the death of everyone on Earth is not an option. We must as a species somehow survive. Mei, I will trust your judgement. I pray you have the strength to do what must be done. I do not envy your task," Abir said softly, then patted Mei on the shoulder as he walked to the door.

"Good luck, girl," John said.

Stephan said. "Mei, if I can help in any way, let me know."

Each man hugged Mei on his way out of the conference room. After the room was empty, Mei returned to the table and looked at a map of the world on her computer.

CHAPTER 32

AFTER THE GROUP LEFT MEI in the MIT conference room, five of the men said goodbye and went their separate ways. But John decided to walk around the campus, and after an hour he sat down on a bench next to a small lake. He gazed at the ducks and geese that floated by and thought back to Alabama and the ponds and lakes they had there.

He wondered how he could ever go back to that place and tell those people who believed in him and believed in the Lord how it had all been a lie and maybe, just maybe, he had been part of that lie. He also realized he could never be part of any plan that would lead to any of those folks being killed, or eliminated, or disposed of, or any damn thing like that. He knew what he wanted to have happen. It would be best for everybody that way. Everyone would be gone, and if the Lord was willin', it would start all over again someday.

He thought of the small trailer that he, his brother Bobby, and his two sisters lived in with their mama after their daddy had been killed in a bar fight when John was six. When John was nine, he learned how his mama fed and clothed her four hungry mouths when he walked in on her after all the kids had been shooed out of the trailer earlier in the day and told to visit friends for the rest of the afternoon.

As he stood outside her bedroom, he looked through the crack in the door and saw a young white sailor boy whose white uniform was draped over a nearby chair. All he had on was his black socks and shiny black shoes. He was moving real fast on top of his mama, and she was making sounds he had never heard before. She was being hurt.

John ran toward the sailor after he had grabbed a baseball bat from near the door that his mama kept there for protection. Before the sailor could react or defend himself, John hit him in the head four times, fracturing his skull and spewing blood over his mama and the sailor's white uniform.

Raising the bat to hit the sailor yet again, his mama yelled "John, stop, John! Oh my Lord, what have you done? You done killed this man!"

"But mama, he was hurtin' you," John explained as he gasped for breath.

"Oh my God. What are we gonna do now? You done a real bad thing, boy."

"But mama…"

"Hush now, boy, I got to think."

His mama's plan was to wait until dark when all the nosy neighbors were asleep, then take the sailor out back, beyond the tall grass, past the pine woods and all the way to that nasty old pond.

At 11:30 that night, after his brother Bobby and his sisters had been told of the "accident," the sailor was wrapped in an old blue blanket, and the family dragged him out the back door and lugged him nearly a quarter mile to the pond, a place they had always been warned to stay away from, especially at night.

The area around the pond had a musty smell of rotting pine needles, mold, and decaying flesh. There were sounds of frogs, and repeated deep snorting sounds from the back of the pond that scared John. Mosquitoes buzzed around the sweating family after their long trek into the darkness, with only an old nearly dead flashlight to guide them that emitted a pale yellow glow.

Near the edge of the water, his mama and Bobby unrolled the sailor, and the body tumbled half in and half out of the water. When Bobby tried to push him completely into the pond, his mama said, "Boy, get away from that water right now. C'mon, y'all, we need to go on home."

Soon after they turned away from the pond to return to the trailer, John heard more snorting and a splashing of tails as six alligators tore the sailor apart and removed nearly all evidence.

They next morning John awoke from a bad dream and had his oatmeal breakfast with his family before going to town to shop for a new pair of jeans for Bobby. From that day forward, no one in the family ever spoke of the young sailor man again. It was as though what had happened that night had never happened at all.

Over time, John himself wondered if it really had happened. Many nights, John would think of the sailor, but as the years went on, he realized it had been a nighttime illusion. It was just a bad nightmare.

For several years, the visions of the sailor went away. But when he was thirteen, he again had the terrifying nightmare about the young man in the white uniform and shiny black shoes. But this time when he got up for his oatmeal breakfast, John went into the living room and told Bobby about what he had dreamed. He told him it was just like the ones he had had all those years before. For the first time, he asked Bobby about the sailor because Bobby had been in the dream too. "What the hell you takin' about, boy? There weren't no sailor in here, ever. You crazy."

It was if Bobby had lifted a hundred pound weight off John's shoulders. *It had all been a damn dream.* A kid's dream. All those sleepless nights then waking up all sweaty and scared and feeling sick. John shook his head and laughed to himself how he let a dream mess him up so bad.

For the first time in four years, John decided to go back to that place in his dream. To face it down and kill that dream once and for all. Laugh in its damn face. When he neared the turbid pond, a familiar smell came back to him. A smell of rot.

He stood in the sand and looked across the nearly black water.

Twenty yards into the water, he could see the eyes of a gator as it basked in the shallow water keeping cool in the mid-day sun. In the shade of weeping willows, he could see several other gators and they all seemed to be looking at him. They too had been in his little kid's nightmare.

He reached down and grabbed a rock from the wet sand and threw it toward the biggest one whose eyes still crested just above the water line. His missed his target but the splash of the water made the gator slowly slip below the surface leaving only bubbles in his wake.

John felt empowered by the vanquishing of his stupid kid's dream and his newfound ability to make the gators disappear under the water. He picked up more rocks and threw them as hard as he could. After a dozen throws, he decided he would find a real big rock and heave it as far as he could and make a real big splash in the murky pond before he left. He saw a white rock buried in the sand and kicked at it to loosen it from the muck. He moved it with his foot, got a good grip on it, and pulled.

What emerged from the sand was a femur bone, attached to an ankle bone, attached to a dirty, mud-filled, no longer shiny black shoe. As John stared in horror at what he had pulled from the muck, an eight-foot gator slithered silently out of the pond and sprinted toward John. Helpless, John flung the bones and shoe at the gator and prepared for a final nightmare.

Three feet short of John, the gator hungrily snapped up the bones and shoe and returned to the pond, his lunch in tow.

John sat on the sand for several moments in shock over what had just occurred. Finally, he saw a half dozen ripples in the pond and realized the posse of gators he had seen earlier in the shade of the weeping willow was headed toward him. He scrambled to his feet but fell face first into the sand, knocking the breath from his lungs.

As one, the five gators saw their opportunity and charged out of the water toward John. He crawled for a few feet but then heard the snorts from the gators like he had heard that night. He got to his feet and sprinted like a young man who was being chased by five gators. He sprinted through the pine woods, into the tall grass, and finally, into his trailer.

CHAPTER 33

"IT WEREN'T NO DREAM, MAMA," he shouted as he tried to catch his breath after his quarter-mile sprint.

His mother was watching her favorite afternoon soap. "Hush, boy, I'm watchin' my story."

"Mama, Bobby said it was a dream. But it weren't no dream."

After a laundry detergent commercial came on, his mother turned and asked, "What the hell you sayin' about a dream?"

"The sailor mama, I killed that sailor man and I just found his bones down at the pond."

"Oh Lord. That was a long time ago, boy. Don't be bringin' up that story to folks around here. They quit lookin' for that sailor."

"But mama, I killed that sailor and like the reverend said, if you kill somebody you'll go to hell and burn forever. I don't want to burn forever, mama!"

"Johnny, you was just trying to protect your mama, you didn't mean to hurt that man. The Lord knows that."

"No, I did wrong and killed a man, and now the devil is gonna wait for me in hell like the reverend says."

"All right Johnny, if that's how you feel, the only thing you can do is become a reverend yourself and promise the Lord you'll serve him until you die. That way he'll forgive you and let you into heaven."

"Is that really true, mama?"

"Yep, it's true, boy. You serve the Lord and that'll fix things."

CHAPTER 34

ON A CLOUDLESS, SPECTACULARLY BEAUTIFUL day on Biscayne Bay, David was drinking cocktails on the back of his yacht with three other men. All wore swimsuits and printed shirts, had dark tans and cool sunglasses. On the bow of the boat, were four spectacularly beautiful young women who lay topless in the sun, their bodies glistening with Hawaiian Tropic.

"We took a big step today," David said.

"Is she in or not?" the man in the green floral shirt said.

"I think she is," David said.

"I figured it would be her or Stephan," The blue floral-shirted man said.

"She's stronger than Stephan," David noted.

"What's next?" the man in the yellow shirt asked.

"I'm taking her to Aspen to learn the process."

"Mixing business with pleasure, old boy?" Blue shirt asked with smile.

"As smart as she is, she'll learn quickly. I doubt she'll be in the mood for much pleasure."

"Why are we waiting another ten months? Our people are ready now," Green shirt said.

"She wouldn't agree to anything but a simultaneous event. She also decided to use the multibeam approach. The destruction of the asteroid will be the method to get people clustered together in huge numbers. The downside is that will take some time to organize. But the upside is that I think the total may even exceed what we planned for. I thought that was worth the wait."

"Maybe you're right. The interest is building, and I think our estimates could be conservative. But if we can free up more opportunities it will pay off in the long run." Blue shirt noted.

"You cleared everything with the Alliance?" Yellow shirt asked.

"Sure. But we're not doing any of the reduction so there was no issue," David explained.

The other three men smiled at the prospect of another large annual bonus. That potential financial windfall prompted all four of the men to grab their drinks and join their female companions on the bow of the ship. It looked like a very promising Sunday afternoon for all concerned.

CHAPTER 35

IN HER TOWNHOUSE IN BOSTON, Mei sat at her computer and studied maps, charts, and photos of various cultures around the world. Her cell rang. She saw it was Stephan. "Stephan! You back in California?"

"No, I'm down here in your lobby. Can I come up?"

"Sure. I'll buzz you in."

After a hug and small talk, Mei and Stephan sat on her patio and drank wine. "Mei, I'm fine with you making the decisions that have to be made. But you may need help with research or someone to bounce ideas off of, so I wanted you to know, I'm just a call away. I'll help any way I can."

"Stephan, I appreciate the offer, but I need to make these decisions myself. It's not fair to bring someone else into the process."

"I can't make you take my help, but I'll be available to you whenever you need anything. If you change your mind and need a sounding board, just call me. Okay?"

After another hour of talking about everything except what faced Mei, Stephan got up to leave.

"Thanks, Stephan. I appreciate you stopping by and for your consideration. For a rich guy, you're not all bad."

"Well, I was in the neighborhood and all."

Stephan and Mei walked to her door, hugged, and Stephan kissed Mei on the cheek.

"By the way, when this is all over, I want you to know upfront that I'll be hitting on you big time," Stephan said.

"I…"

"Before you say anything, have you ever been hit on by a guy worth three billion? I can be pretty persuasive."

"I'll look forward to that," Mei said.

Several moments after Stephan walked out her door, Mei opened it and saw the elevator doors close. She had wanted to run to the doors to say something to Stephan before he left, but she decided it could keep. If she could not do what she had to do in the next few months, nothing would matter anyway.

CHAPTER 36

AS THE ELEVATOR DOORS STARTED to close, Stephan reached out and was about to put his arm between the doors. He wanted to go back and tell Mei how he really felt about her. How he had flown all night just to see her. How she was the most brilliant and beautiful woman he had ever met. But then he didn't. He wasn't sure why he didn't, he just didn't.

Maybe it was because he didn't want to complicate a life that was already more complicated than perhaps any life on the planet had ever been. What Mei faced was something that would undoubtedly change her even if she survived. And he intuitively knew it was possible, even likely, that she would end up taking her own life for what she had been tasked to do.

Until his diagnosis with liver cancer, it appeared that Stephan Connor had been born under a lucky star. All-American high school athlete in three sports, academic All-American at Stanford, Rhodes Scholar, millionaire at twenty-six, and billionaire at thirty-two. He was also movie-star good-looking and dated movie stars. He anonymously donated to homes for abused women and children and to animal shelters around the country. All things considered, Stephan had his shit together.

He had decided that when he turned forty, he was going to run for president to improve his resume; besides, he liked D.C. But then he was told he was going to die. Then he was told he wasn't. Then he was told the world could end in a year, but it wouldn't end if he would help kill a few billion people. In short, for all he had accomplished in his life, he was pretty fucked up, as was the rest of the world.

Maybe that was why he wanted to go back and talk to Mei and let her know how he really felt, but he concluded that would be selfish. He wanted someone in his life, but not now. What would be the point? So they could die together in a few months?

At the controls of his G-650 on his flight back to California, he concluded that he had never had the competition for a woman as he was certain he had with David for Mei. He could read the body language between the two of them and figured David would use his alien wiles, whatever they happened to be, to make Mei his, at least for a while.

Stephan had never met a guy who was at least as good-looking as he was, had arguably more money, the cachet of being from another fucking planet, and even a cooler aircraft. Pretty tough competition. But Stephan was, among other things, patient; and when he set his mind to it, he always got what he wanted. He only hoped that the woman he wanted would want him after this was all over. But mostly, he hoped, she would still be alive.

CHAPTER 37

TWO DAYS LATER IN THE Aspen house, Mei and David sat in his office next to what looked like a traditional computer keyboard. It wasn't. There was a small remote control-like attachment on the side. David picked up the device, hit a button, and a floor-to-ceiling orange three-dimensional array appeared between him and Mei. It displayed a rotating Earth.

"You can highlight any part of the globe you like—just move it like this." David pointed to Europe, and a beam emitted from the device. In less than a second, a large twenty-four-inch segment of the globe representing Europe appeared and levitated above David and Mei. "Here, try it," David said.

Mei took the small device and pointed the beam at Asia. The image moved from the rotating globe and slowly rotated in the air presenting a three-dimensional 360-degree view of the continent.

"After you pick a general location, you can home in on smaller areas by aiming the beam where you want to…"

"Kill a few billion people?"

"Yes, Mei. To save this planet, billions must die, so billions can live. If you're not up to this task, we're wasting our time here."

"This is an emotionless exercise for you, isn't? You're like Mr. Spock."

"I see this as an opportunity to save a planet and billions of its inhabitants. I've grown very fond of Earth and even some of its inhabitants and want to see it survive. It's not that I'm unemotional; it's just that for the moment you and I need to be pragmatic. Billions of people can be saved, and the Earth can flourish if we, I mean, you, can do the right thing."

"So killing this many people causes you no angst? No sleepless nights?"

"A planet and every living thing on it turned to ash would create more angst for me. Because it would be a waste of everything that has ever occurred on Earth. Every accomplishment. Every medical breakthrough. Every piece of art. Every note of music. Every written word. Every act of heroism and self-sacrifice over thousands of years all wiped out. Erased like none of it ever happened. Is that what you want?"

"Of course not, but the idea of pushing a button and ending billions of lives…"

"Would you push a button to save billions of lives?"

Mei stared at David for several moments. "I want to meet your superiors," she said.

"That's not possible."

"Why not?"

"I'm the representative for the Alliance and have been given my orders, and I have given you your options. That's how it works."

Mei continued to stare at David for several more moments as the levitating maps of Asia and Europe separated them as surely as David's words to Mei had.

Finally, with a hardness in her voice, Mei asked, "Okay, how do I kill three billion people?"

With no hesitation, David said, "By using this." He closed the levitating maps and moved next to Mei. He replaced the maps with an image of the moon.

"The moon...?"

"It's has been an armed observation and monitoring post for centuries. It's how we learned about your cultures, mores, and languages. It's from there that we've protected you from space debris for thousands of years. Those are the same beams you'll activate, and they will come from inside hundreds of craters."

For the next thirty minutes, David instructed Mei on how to access the high-powered beams that would, on her command, vaporize billions of her fellow Earth citizens. She learned quickly.

"Ready to try it?" David asked.

"Try what? You mean kill an innocent person? Now?"

"I can't be here with you when you make your decisions and direct the beams. So, we should be sure you're comfortable with the process."

"Why not another vacant building? Or an iceberg or a tree?"

"Why not all three?" David suggested, grinning.

Mei took the device from David and opened the rotating orange globe once again. She began to initiate the process she had learned. She made a wrong move. "No, this is how..."

"I got it, I got it...let me do it," Mei said impatiently.

Mei corrected her mistake. She selected Ohio and picked out a grove of dead trees in a woods outside Ashtabula. She highlighted the trees and hit "Send." Within a second, the grove of trees that had been levitating in front of her on the screen disappeared. "My god, there's hardly any lag time," she said.

"Good job."

"How about an iceberg?"

"Have at it," David said.

Mei was successful again. David then took the device from Mei. "This is always fun."

After a few buttons were pushed, a wheat field in England was levitating in front of Mei. Seconds later, an intricate geometric design appeared in the field.

"So that's how…"

"Cool, huh? Makes people nuts."

Over the next hour, Mei and David took turns "testing" the eradication process. They took out junked cars in Russia, an abandoned building in Fresno, and assorted edifices in Chernobyl. Mei became very proficient in the process. Even better than David.

"You are a natural, my dear."

"It's like a video game," Mei said.

Later that night at the Biltmore Hotel in Coral Gables, Mei and David had dinner. "I think you should just stay with me until this is all over."

"I don't think so," Mei said.

"Why not?

"Aren't you married? I saw pictures of you and a woman with two children on the boat."

"No. I'm not married."

"What about the pictures?"

"I have two children and am close with their mother but…"

"You make her sound like breeding stock."

"In my world, marriage is not a concept we believe in. It's about *wanting* to be with someone, not *having* to be with them."

"How modern."

"Why haven't you married?" David asked.

"Never had the time. Or I guess, the interest."

"When this is all done, you'll have more time. Everyone will. Things will be different."

"How will things be different?" Mei asked.

"Life will be easier, people will live longer…"

"You mean you'll provide cures for illnesses?"

"Sure. Why not? The population will be greatly reduced, and Earth will begin to heal itself. Within months you'll see that the air and water will be cleaner. Everyone will have excellent housing, medical care, good food, clothing, and won't have to worry about making money to survive. They'll have time to do anything they want."

"Sounds too good to be…"

"Cultures on other planets have lived this way for thousands of years. You guys are just a bit late to the party. Some wine?"

"Ahh…after what happened last time, I don't think wine is a good idea."

"What happened last time was a wonderful experience, at least for me."

"That sounds like a man talking."

"Okay, let's pretend it didn't happen. And no wine tonight. How about we go to my place on Fisher Island, sit by the pool and talk. You then go to your own room, I go to mine, and I fix you breakfast in the morning?"

CHAPTER 38

THE NEXT MORNING MEI AWOKE in the king-size bed alone. She was wearing a man's cotton T-shirt with a University of Miami logo on the front that David had given her. She instinctively looked to the other side of the bed. It was empty, and the pillow and bedspread were undisturbed. She got up and walked to the mirror and ran her fingers through her hair then opened the top of her shirt and saw a faint bruise on her neck. She moved her hands over her breasts and then downward as if she were feeling for pain. Was it a faint pain she felt? Or was it her imagination?

On the patio of David's Fisher Island home, he was reading the morning paper at a glass table. Mei walked into pool area dressed in navy blue shorts, a white midriff top, and sandals.

"Okay to borrow these clothes I found in the bathroom?" she asked.

"You're not borrowing them; I bought them for you."

"Pretty sure I'd stay, huh?"

"Let's say I was hopeful."

Mei sat down at the Brown Jordan table, grabbed a bagel, and spread it with cream cheese.

"Coffee or tea?" David asked.

"Tea, please."

"How about my suggestion from last night?"

"What suggestion?"

"You know, you staying here till this is all over."

Mei looked around at her luxurious and beautiful surroundings. She saw the yacht docked a few yards away and said, "Well, if it was a nicer place, I might consider it."

"You should see my joint in Carmel."

"I admit being alone now is tough. I think about all those..."

"Trying to do something like this on your own would be almost impossible, for anyone."

"How do we handle... the other stuff, you know, you and me?" Mei asked.

"Look, I have too big an ego to try to force anything with you. You'll get no pressure from me, I promise. If you want to keep it all business, then all business it will be. You can draw those boundaries. I want you to want me. I don't want to talk you into anything. If you decide you don't want me, then I guess I'll just suck it up and hope that in this big, wide universe there's another beautiful, caring, sexy, brilliant, size 4, physicist waiting for me."

Mei stared at David seriously for several moments. Then she slowly shook her head and said, "No, I am the *only* size 4."

David broke out in laughter.

CHAPTER 39

MEI'S PARENTS HAD ADOPTED HER from an orphanage in Beijing after a year of legal wrangling and the payments of a series of bribes to local and regional governmental authorities. They also had to sign agreements that they would never have any of their own children; if they did, they would lose both that child and Mei.

While Mei's parents were unemotional and not physically demonstrative, they loved her and devoted themselves to her homeschooling including the development of her musical and artistic skills. But it was her academic skills that astounded her parents who were both college- educated professors who still taught classes at the college level in math and science.

By the time she was seven, Mei had not only mastered Mandarin, but she was also proficient in English and French and could fake it in Spanish. She had an astounding comprehension of mathematics and science, and her parents recognized that she was a prodigy who needed to go to Europe or the United States to further her educational development.

But Mei was also very opinionated and wasn't sure what she wanted to do when she grew up. At first, she wanted to become a doctor and see what was inside people's bodies. Find out how they worked and why they didn't work sometimes. But then she learned she would have to cut up cats, dogs, or guinea pigs at some point and that was when she changed her mind about a career in medicine.

From time to time, she thought about becoming a professor like her parents but while she didn't tell them for fear of hurting their feelings, that sounded boring to her. Then she went through her "I want to be a concert pianist" stage, which she could have done given her musical gifts. Then there was her "I want to be a lawyer" stage after she saw Atticus Finch defend Tom Robinson. But no matter what her career plans were at any moment, she never stopped looking at the stars every night. They made her wonder and imagine what it all meant. Were there people on other planets looking back at her at that exact moment?

When her parents announced that Mei had been accepted to a prestigious private school in Boston for the academically gifted and would be leaving for the United States as soon as her visa was in order, Mei accepted the news with the same stoicism as the news had been given to her by her mother and father. It was as if she knew this was going to happen sooner or later, and she was following a script that had been written for her life by someone else.

The day she left for America, her parents took her to the airport, and she was turned over to an airline official who would see to it that she arrived in Boston safe and sound. After some uncomfortable moments of awkward good-byes, Mei ran back into the arms of her mother and began to sob. Her father knelt and embraced her as tears ran down his face. "You must study hard," he said. Her mother couldn't speak, but held her daughter close until the Air Asian official said, "Please, we must go now."

From the day she arrived in Boston, Mei was an academic superstar. It was not only her comprehension and retention that impressed her teachers; it was her tenacity in overcoming problems and her single-mindedness that set her apart from the rest of her classmates, all of whom were brilliant in their own right. Mei was simply more brilliant.

After she obtained her undergraduate degree from Harvard, she went to Cal Tech for her master's before obtaining her PhD in astrophysics from Princeton. A week before she graduated, she received an offer from MIT for a full professorship. When she accepted the position, she thought back to the time she thought such a career would be boring.

The day in her office when she had picked up and read the invitation to Aspen from David, she sensed that if she was indeed bored, that would soon change. She had even thought at the time if what she and her colleagues had learned about the asteroid only days before, was somehow and in some way linked to David's invitation. But how could it be? But then it was. It seemed everything was linked.

CHAPTER 40

AFTER HER DECISION TO MOVE in with David prior to the *event*, Mei and David were together virtually every day. They spent time in Carmel, Aspen, Miami, Paris, and Rome. David even taught Mei to fly his "toy." She particularly enjoyed seeing how fast she could circle the globe at the equator. Her record was twenty-one minutes. He did it in fourteen and on more than one occasion made some derogatory quips about women drivers. Mei responded by giving him the finger.

In early March, snow could be seen on the slopes through the windows at David's Aspen home. Mei was reading *Time* magazine next to a warm glowing fireplace, sipping hot chocolate while David was working at his computer "Want to see it?" he asked and motioned to Mei to come look at his computer screen.

"See what?"

"Big Ben. Its orbital path is bringing it in sight."

Mei looked over David's shoulder. On the screen she saw the massive boulder tumbling through space.

"It'll be visible in the night sky in a week," David said.

"It doesn't look that big," Mei said.

"It's not compared to the rest of space, but its size is equal to the distance between LA and Orange County. It could make a pretty good-sized hole in the Earth."

"Do we have an exact date and time for when…?"

"April 14 would be the best date given the current trajectory, angle, Jupiter's gravitational pull, and the eventual speed of Big Ben. I'll have an exact time in the next few days, but it looks like around 3:20 p.m. eastern daylight time. "

"What do we do between now and then?" Mei asked.

"Given his popularity and credibility, I suggest that Robert call a press conference at the United Nations next week to announce the best locations for viewing the destruction of Big Ben. It will be a worldwide event that will be unlike anything anyone has ever seen," David said.

"I agree. I'll call Robert today and get him moving on that front."

"David, what about afterward? How does he or any of us explain what happened to all those people?"

"Initially, the only explanation that will suffice, and the only one that will prevent riots after the fact, is to report that it was a tragic malfunction. We will say that the asteroid was destroyed as promised. As a result, the planet and every living thing on it was saved from total extinction. However, we will also explain that the beam that hit the asteroid ricocheted off the tumbling rock then unexpectedly and tragically splintered. People all over the planet were killed by a thousand fractured beams that hit Earth."

"People won't believe that story. Especially if the splintered beam I launch only hits places where millions of people congregated," Mei said.

"That's why I have arranged that several thousand more beams, separate from the beams that you will launch, will hit the Earth at the exact moment the asteroid is destroyed. The beams I launch will be in unpopulated locations as well as some areas where physical damage can be documented but no lives put in danger. Don't forget that neither I nor anyone else on my team can be responsible for the lives of anyone on Earth."

"You didn't tell me about those additional beams before."

"You had enough on your plate to worry about," David said.

"I still wonder if people will buy that story."

"I think they will. First of all, you told me that not all of the places where millions will congregate are on your list to be hit," David said.

"That's right," Mei said.

"Good. That will create a sense of randomness relative to the locations that will be hit. Eventually, most people will just say "shit happens" especially if they didn't lose a loved one. But despite the loss of life, people all over the Earth will, in a short period of time, realize how much better their lives are and accept what's told to them. Besides, there won't be anyone to contradict our story, no one believable anyway."

"What about us? What will happen with us after all this is over?" Mei asked.

"Are you happy with me?"

"As happy as I can be under the circumstances."

"The circumstances will only get better. I love you and want to spend time with you."

"A mass murderer?" Mei said.

"A heroine."

CHAPTER 41

ROBERT MITCHELL HAD NEVER LONGED to be president of the United States. In fact, he never wanted be a congressman, a senator, or even the attorney that he became early in his career. As a kid, he wanted to be a cowboy. Then the idea of being in a rock band and driving a Harley was on the list of "cool things" he wanted to try. But despite himself, he learned that high school, college, and even law school was easy for him. When he read something, it stuck. While his classmates studied and "crammed," Robert just read, or even skimmed, and he retained all of it.

His intellectual gifts were noticed by political types, and Robert found himself on what appeared to be an inevitable track to the White House.

While holding what was arguably the most political of all political positions, Robert was not a dyed-in-the-wool Democrat. When possible, he listened to the other side and even gave serious thought to naming a Republican as vice president until receiving major pushback from his party.

Prior to taking office in his first term, Robert had vowed on the campaign trial that he would investigate government files and release whatever he learned to the American public about UFOs and possible life on other planEts. That fact is, he didn't learn much.

What he did learn was that even the president would be kept in the dark about such subjects if it were feared that the information would be released as Robert had promised. Despite his inability to confirm reports of UFOs, aliens, or other fanciful stories, Robert had gained the trust of a broad swath of the American people.

Two weeks before the asteroid would enter Earth's atmosphere, former POTUS Robert Mitchell addressed the General Assembly of the United Nations.

"Ladies and gentlemen. Over the past ten and a half months, our world has undertaken and endured what can only be called historic, unprecedented, and in some cases admittedly chaotic change. Change that no one, including me, thought possible. While those changes were absolutely required to sustain the people of Earth and the existence of our planet, people from all over the globe have come together in a unity unlike anything we as a civilization have ever witnessed before. Palestinian and Jew. Shia and Shiite. Black, white, brown, yellow, and red, North and South Korea, Russia, and the United States and hundreds more have come together in an effort to recraft life as we know it on the planet we all call home."

As Robert spoke, billions of people all over the world watched and listened to a man they intuitively knew and trusted. A man they had seen on the world stage for nearly forty years. People around the world may have at times disagreed with Robert's politics, but they believed him when he spoke, even if they did not always like his message. But that day, he delivered a stirring message of global unity that the entire world welcomed with relief, hope, and unbridled enthusiasm.

"The world's largest corporations have merged and created ways and means of delivering products to people all over the world who are in need. Political leaders have dropped party affiliations, leaders of world powers have agreed to erase national boundaries allowing free movement across the world."

Political, and religious leaders around the world who had originally pushed back hard on making the changes within their groups and organizations had come around to the message that Robert and the rest of the group of seven had been delivering over the past several months. The message was simple: change or perish.

"Yet all these changes would not have been possible if it were not for religious leaders around the globe coming together under a unified banner and committing to a new international faith based on humanism rather than dogma. The melding together of these religious groups, including their significant financial resources, emphasizes those common beliefs found in all religious texts, including freedom from persecution, equal rights, and the idea that all people of this planet deserve and will receive food, medical care, education, a living wage, and the opportunity to, through their own individual initiative, creativity, and intellectual capabilities, find unlimited success, growth, and development."

While Robert had focused his message of change on the international political front, Stephan and Abir took on the challenge of explaining to the international business community how they could make as much as they had before if geographic market barriers were eliminated between nations. Those business leaders bought it. Father Peña and Reverend John spoke to religious groups and introduced the concept of humanism over theology, even though John could never bring himself to relate the "truth" as told to him by David. At the same time, Billy and Mei spoke to the scientific community around the world and explained how life on Earth would improve dramatically after the asteroid was destroyed with the help of our new intergalactic partners.

"What we have accomplished as a global community over the last

nearly eleven months is hold up our end of the bargain with a group of intergalactic partners who will now protect us from what would have been certain annihilation. This scientific fact has now been confirmed by every scientist in the world. In fact, in the southern sky every night we can now see that very object that would have otherwise destroyed our planet."

While there were hundreds of small groups representing millions of people around the world who defiantly fought against any kind of change, their voices were drowned out by the overwhelming number of people who welcomed the kinds of changes that the group of seven were advocating.

"Two weeks from today, Earth, with the help of our neighbors from other worlds, will avoid destruction. This event will mark a new beginning for everyone on Earth. A beginning that includes our planet becoming part of an intergalactic community we never knew existed."

The prospect of becoming part of an intergalactic family was initially viewed with trepidation by some and utter terror by others. Yet, there were also people from cultures all around the world who welcomed it. Many claimed that they had known all along that this was the way it was in the universe. It was indeed a family, something that as living, sentient beings, we were all part of. Something to be excited about, not feared.

"In the months following the destruction of what all of us now call Big Ben, the people of Earth will be introduced to those who have saved our planet. We will be shown miraculous things that will make our lives better, safer, and infinitely easier. All this begins in two weeks, on April 14 at precisely 3:19 p.m. eastern daylight time, when the asteroid that would have ended life on our planet will be destroyed by an advanced civilization that had no obligation to do so. I will now outline the details of this event, including the locations to view the destruction of the asteroid. An event like no other in the history of this planet."

Robert's speech was broadcast to every corner of the world where people listened to him describe not only the destruction of Big Ben, but the ushering in of a new world. A world not everyone was anxious to be part of. Before his speech had ended that day, more than 200,000 people around the world had committed suicide.

"Two weeks from today everyone on Earth can see the power of the Alliance when it destroys the asteroid only seconds before it would

have killed every living thing on our planet. By assembling at one of the nearly one thousand worldwide locations that will be described on the internet, radio, TV, and in newspapers around the globe, you will see a spectacular sight that will usher in a new chapter of human development."

At the conclusion of his speech, the audience at the U.N. rose as one, in enthusiastic applause and cheers for what they had just heard. Robert looked at the adoring crowd and produced a small smile, then waved to the audience. Later, in a phone conversation to Stephan, he said, "I felt like I wanted to scream the truth into the camera that I was setting up a large portion of the world to be erased from the face of the Earth. Sometimes I think all of us going together is the right option after all."

"I guess we've all had those thoughts, Robert. Who knows maybe that will be what Mei ultimately decides is the best way to go."

"I don't want to know in advance. I want her to make the decision and whatever happens, happens. Do you think she has made a firm decision yet?"

"Knowing Mei. I would say yes. Only she knows if anyone will be alive on this planet on April 15."

CHAPTER 42

OVER THE NEXT WEEK, NEWSPAPERS, the internet, radio, and TV headlines gave details about the destruction of the asteroid and the locations where it could be best seen. There were also worldwide riots by some religious groups who condemned the destruction of the asteroid, saying it was a message from God. Signs proclaimed *Let Us Die Together as Christians. Death Before No God. God Will Save Us. Allah IS the Answer.* One sign took a different view: *Fuck This Place, Time We Move On.*

Daily demonstrations continued throughout the world in the days leading up to the April 14 destruction of the asteroid. Over 1.5 million more suicides were reported including entire congregations of churches drinking poison at the same time, worshippers in mosques setting off explosions killing everyone inside, families jumping off bridges to their deaths as they held hands, parents shooting their children then themselves.

Then in the first week in April, the suicides stopped. It appeared that those who had killed themselves were a segment of society that believed what was to come in the new world was so frightening that they would not and could not become part of it. Those who chose to take a chance on something new looked forward to an event that would, according to the former U.S. president, change their lives for the better. Those people waited with anticipation and gazed at Big Ben in the night sky as it roared toward Earth.

CHAPTER 43

IN HIS FISHER ISLAND HOME the day before the arrival of Big Ben and the deaths of billions of people around the world, David and Mei sat in the family room and watched the worldwide reactions on TV.

"You realize I can't be with you tomorrow?" David said.

"I know. Stephan called, and the rest of the group will be on a conference call with me to monitor as many sites as we can. All except John. He seems to have vanished."

"I'm glad the rest of the group is helping you."

"There will be no pain?" Mei asked for the hundredth time.

"None. You have my word. What are the latest estimates of attendance at the sites?"

"Over two billion."

"And the rest?"

"I took Robert's advice and decided to adjust the population equally in every major country in the world with my site selections. It seemed like the fairest approach."

"Have you set the coordinates for all the sites?" David asked.

"I have input everything over the last few days. There are nearly one thousand locations."

"Then once you enable the system tomorrow afternoon, you just need to hit "Send" and..."

"I know, I know, and billions of people will cease to exist."

"That's better than all the people," David said.

"I wonder."

The internet and TV continued to show images of peaceful demonstrations around the world. There were signs welcoming and thanking Earth's intergalactic partners who were going to save the planet. Millions of people around the world began their pilgrimages to the locations that had been described. Most were groups of joyous people looking forward to a new world. A world many had defined as heaven. Heaven on Earth. A new Earth.

Later that night Mei lay in bed with David who slept soundly. Mei was unable to sleep and instead stared at the ceiling, her heart pounding in her chest. She tried to calm herself. She feared she was having a heart attack and then what would happen to all those people she could have saved?

Finally giving up on sleep, she got up and walked out the sliding glass door to the veranda that encircled David's mansion.

Mei looked out over Biscayne Bay and could see downtown Miami. The site was beautiful and calm. As she stared into the night, her cell phone buzzed in vibration mode. Billy had sent her a text. "Mei--The fucking numbers are off. I'm checking them again. Call me now."

Mei prepared to respond to Billy's text. In the distance, David had gotten out of bed and stared at Mei in the darkness. He came up behind her and placed his hands on her shoulders.

"Oh! You scared me." Mei said.

"Sorry, honey. Not surprised you can't sleep." David saw Mei's cell on the table. Messages this time of night?"

"It was a text from Billy. Something about the numbers not being right."

"What numbers aren't right?"

"He didn't say."

"Maybe it was the estimates for attendance tomorrow at the sites."

"Maybe. I'm going to grab my robe. I'll be right back. You want anything?"

"How about a bottle of water?" David said.

Mei left the veranda and returned to the house. Mei's phone vibrated again. David read the message from Billy; "Something's fucked up. We have to talk." David typed, "I'll call in AM. I need some sleep." Seconds later: "No... we need to talk now. I'm calling." Mei's phone vibrated with an "incoming call" alert. David picked up Mei's phone and placed it next to his. He typed in a message on his phone, waited several seconds, and hit "Send." Seconds later Mei returned to the veranda with a robe and two bottles of water.

"I need to call Billy and see what's up with him."

"At this hour?"

"He's obviously awake...besides none of us will be sleeping tonight anyway."

"Okay...but before you do, I want you to know how proud I am of you. What you have undertaken is something most people on this planet could not do." David moved to Mei and put his arms around her and kissed her. She didn't respond to his kiss. Instead she moved away from him and picked up her cell phone from the table.

"I really need to call Billy and see what he was talking about."

"Go ahead. I'll wait for you inside."

David returned to the bedroom. Mei looked at her phone screen but the latest text from Billy and the text sent by David were not there. Nor was the notice of Billy's call. All she saw was Billy's original text: *The fucking numbers are off. I'm checking them again.*

Mei dialed Billy's number. No answer. She tried again. No answer. She left a voice mail.

"Hey...what's up? Thought you wanted to talk. I'll be up all night— just call."

Mei set the phone on the table and sat in a lounge chair in the dark, waiting for Billy's call. Despite herself, she dozed off. She was awakened by the sunrise. She checked her phone for messages from Billy. There were none. She walked back into the bedroom. David wasn't there. There was a note on the bed: *Be strong... I love you. D.*

Unable to sleep or eat, Mei wandered around the house and pool area all morning, biding her time until 3:19:00 p.m., the precise time David had calculated that the asteroid would be vaporized. Every few minutes she checked the four clocks in the house that she had set to Greenwich Mean Time. For some reason, time seemed to be moving too fast--like a skier careening downhill out of control. Mei felt the pressure in her chest increase as the minute hands on the clock appeared to gain speed.

At 1:00 p.m. she looked out onto Biscayne Bay; for the first time it was completely empty. She turned on the TV and saw that people from around the world were already in place at the predetermined sites.

The crowds were festive as people jostled to find the best locations. Most wore sunglasses, many had folding chairs and beverage coolers, and others had lugged barbecue grills making the locations look like enormous tailgate parties. There was a lot of beer.

Some crowds were in darkness; some in daylight. People waved banners and carried signs; others played music. Still others prayed. Mei vomited several times as she watched the crowds from across the globe.

Mei's cell rang. It was Stephan. "You holding up?"

"No. I've been shaking all morning. I'm nauseous too," Mei replied

"What did you expect?"

"Have you spoken to Billy?" Mei asked.

"No. He texted me last night and said he wanted to talk to me, but he didn't answer when I called him back. No response from my text either," Stephan said.

"Same with me. Wonder if he tried any of the others?"

"I don't know. Look, I don't want to add to your concern, but John is missing down in Alabama."

"Missing?" Mei asked.

"I spoke to his wife, and she's frantic. She said John decided to tell his congregation about what was going to happen and warned them to stay away from the gathering spots. She said he went for a walk before going to church and has simply disappeared."

"Have you spoken to Robert, José, or Abir?"

"Yes, they all said they'll be on the call today if you need them."

Mei's phone beeped. It was Robert. "Stephan, Robert's calling. I'll put him on the line with you."

Mei clicked a button, and Robert was connected to the call.

"Oh Robert, glad you're here. Stephan's on the line with us."

"Good. So, anybody making any dinner plans for tomorrow night?"

Getting no answer, Robert continued. "I tried to call Abir and José, but there was no answer."

"We only have fifteen minutes." Stephan said. "It's 3:04."

"Is there any more to discuss?" Robert asked.

"Only the numbers. How can we even remotely gauge how many people are going to be at each site?"Stephan asked.

"We can't, but billions are expected," Robert said. "Mei, are you okay with the process? Is David there to help if need be?"

"The process is simple at this point. All I need to do is to activate the system and push a single button. And David is not allowed to be here. This has to be an action taken by us, not the Alliance."

After several long moments of silence the clock on Mei's wall moved to 3:09.

"Mei, what will people see in the sky?" Stephan asked.

"The asteroid will produce a brilliant light in both the night and day light sky when it enters our atmosphere. At exactly 3:19:00 a beam will vaporize the asteroid. At precisely the same time, 3:19:00, I push my button, and the thousand sites I selected will be hit simultaneously."

"What then?"

"Nothing then. It's all over," Mei answered flatly.

Stephan and Robert were silent, unsure of what to say to Mei so they said nothing and waited.

"It's 3:18," Mei said.

Seconds later from Washington D.C., Robert shouted, "I'm outside. I can see a bright light in the eastern sky. Oh, my God. it's huge!! I can hear a roar!"

At 3:18:12 from California, Stephan said, "I can see it here in L.A. The ground is shaking. I hear it!!"

3:18:16. Mei stared at the computer. Her screen showed a thousand red dots on a world map that were slowly pulsating.

3:18:21. "It's like a second sun!" Stephan said.

3:18:24. "It's deafening here in D.C!"

3:18:31. Mei's hand trembled as it hovered over the Send button.

3:18:38. "It's heading west," Robert said.

3:18:44. "My God, it's enormous!" Stephan said.

3:18:52. Mei's mind cleared, and her hand steadied as she silently counted down the last eight seconds.

3:19:00. A single beam came from the clear blue sky and intercepted the asteroid. It was vaporized in a second.

3:19:00. Over two thousand other beams rain down on Earth hitting uninhabited locations across the planet.

3:19:02. "My God! It's gone! They did it!!" Robert shouted from Washington D.C.

3:19:02 "Unbelievable! It just vanished!" Stephan said from LA, with awe in his voice.

3:19:02. Mei's forefinger touched the Send button.

3:19:05. "Mei, the asteroid is gone. Have you pushed the button? Mei, wait, they already destroyed the asteroid!! You don't have to do it!! Don't do it!!" Robert screamed into the phone.

3:19: 08. "Mei, wait!! It's gone!! Maybe there's another way!!" Stephan yelled.

3:19: 10. Mei's finger continued to hover over the Send button.

3:19:12. "Mei, are you there? The asteroid has been destroyed! If you haven't sent the beams, you don't have to! The danger has passed! Mei, answer me!" Stephan shouted.

3:19:14. "Mei, can you hear me? Don't...?" There were suddenly two simultaneous dial tones as Robert and Stephan were disconnected from the call with Mei.

3:19:15. Mei's finger moved away from the Send button.

3:19:16. Mei continued to stare at the nearly one thousand pulsating red lights indicating the targets that had been locked onto.

3:19:17. Mei pushed the button.

CHAPTER 44

3:19:00. AT THAT PRECISE SECOND, billions of people in a thousand separate locations around the world cheered the destruction of the asteroid and the hope for a new world of which they would all be a part. Their collective futures and euphoria lasted seventeen seconds.

3:19:18. A second later most of those same people were enveloped by a blue-white beam and...gone. There were no screams of pain; in fact there were no sounds at all. There was no explosion, no remnants of bodies. No smoke. No heat. No damage to the ground on which the people had stood.

A man standing by his wife gazing up at the asteroid and seeing it destroyed simply ceased to exist while his wife looked curiously at the spot where her husband had been standing a heartbeat before. *Where had he gone?* she thought. *How strange, he was just here a second ago.*

Like when a tornado completely destroys one house and leaves the one next door untouched, millions of people disappeared in an area the size of Times Square, leaving the people who had been standing next to them unscathed although certainly perplexed. And terrified.

Mei sat at her computer and saw the red dots on her screen blink off. It was such a benign action—billions were dead but the lights on the screen went out with no fanfare, no ominous music, or even an enormous explosion. Mei wasn't sure what she had been expecting, but it wasn't this. Didn't the deaths of billions deserve more drama?

She looked down at her phone and saw calls from Robert and Stephan. Did they hang up or did she? All she could remember was the time of 3:19:00. The time she pushed the Send button. She knew she pushed it because all the red lights were now out. If she hadn't pushed it all those lights would still be on her screen. All those people would still be...

In the background, the TV showed camera shots from around the globe telling two stories; first, of the asteroid's destruction, but then seconds later, of the crowds that had disappeared.

> *"Mark, we're a quarter mile from where an estimated 2.5 million people had gathered in the desert outside Qatar to see the destruction of the asteroid...and...I don't how to say this...but...those people... are gone!"*

> *"I am here outside Las Vegas and what I am about to report is staggering. A crowd estimated at two million people has disappeared after watching the asteroid be destroyed. They are gone. They have simply vanished!"*

"CNN is reporting that a crowd outside of Shanghai estimated at three million is reported...gone. I repeat—more than three million people have utterly disappeared. Even more are reported missing in Beijing."

"This is William Mayer reporting for FOX News from Sao Paulo, Brazil, where untold millions of people are reported missing after..."

Mei clicked off the TV with the remote and shut off her computer. She sat back in her chair and took a drink of water from the bottle on her desk. She rose and walked to a window and looked at the Miami skyline. Everything looked normal. Her cell phone rang. It was Billy. "It wasn't going to hit," he said softly.

"Wha...? What are you talking about, Billy?"

"I said the asteroid wasn't going to hit."

CHAPTER 45

"WHAT ARE YOU TALKING ABOUT? I saw it in the sky on TV, everyone saw it," Mei said without emotion.

"Do you have a slide rule?"

"A slide rule?"

"Yeah, a fucking slide rule. All the computers around the world have been fed the wrong data. It was going to miss the Earth by 53,000 miles. You can figure it out with a slide rule. A fucking slide rule."

"But it was destroyed...they saved the Earth."

"My ass. It would have been a pretty cool flyby, but it was going to miss."

"You're wrong. All the computers showed the path it was going..."

"No, Mei...I'm right. Jupiter's gravitational pull was purposely overstated by someone. Every fucking computer on the planet was fed the wrong data. It was without question going to miss, Mei."

"I don't understand..." The phone connection with Billy went dead. Mei moved to a desk where she had her briefcase. She dumped it out on the floor and found the leather case that held her slide rule from her undergraduate days. She went back to her computer and began to copy data onto a yellow legal tablet.

Over the next several hours, Mei worked feverishly using her calculator, slide rule, and her computer. Day gave way to night. Mei continued at her computer, inputting data. An image of the Earth appeared. Near it, a dotted line representing the path of the asteroid was shown. At first, it appeared the path of the asteroid led to an Earth strike near Portland, Oregon. But a revised computerized path, based on the new information Mei had put into the computer and verified by her slide rule, showed the asteroid missing the Earth by 53,000 miles.

Mei gaped at the computer screen in disbelief and began to tremble. Her cell phone rang. It was David, calling for the fifth time since Big Ben had been destroyed. This time Mei answered.

"It worked!" he said. "Where have you been, I've called you all day?"

"What?" Mei responded hoarsely.

"I talked to the Alliance, and they said you lived up to the bargain. Enough people were eliminated to make them recommend that Earth continue as a viable entity."

"It was going to miss," Mei said softly.

David didn't respond to Mei's statement.

"It was going to miss, David."

"I'll be home in twenty minutes."

Mei dropped her cell on the floor and moved haltingly to the window and looked out onto a moonlit but deserted Biscayne Bay. After several minutes, she moved to the bathroom and stared into the mirror and saw the image of a dazed and exhausted woman looking back at her. She spoke softly to the image, "It was going to miss."

She removed a bottle of sleeping pills from the drawer and stared at them. After she filled a glass with water, she swallowed sixty-one of the pills.

After taking the pills, she went to the bedroom and lay down on the bed with the sliding doors wide open. Her eyes, filled with tears, were open wide for several seconds. Then they slowly closed, and all the pain drifted from her.

CHAPTER 46

Three Years Later

IN THEIR NEW HOME IN Aspen, Mei was asleep in a king-size bed while David read the *Financial Times* in his office. In her dream, Mei saw a blinding flash. A large group of people were staring at her. They smiled, then their faces melted. Mei moaned and turned over in bed. Moments later she slowly opened her eyes. She saw David in his chair in the adjoining room.

"What's for breakfast?" she asked groggily.

"Ever hear of a thing called a tapeworm?" David asked.

"Also known as twins."

"What would the boys like this morning?"

"They are demanding pancakes, sausage, and warm syrup. Some of that special coffee you bought would be nice too."

"Those boys are really getting demanding. Okay, get your butt in the shower, and I'll slave over a hot stove for you."

Mei made a face at David, got out of bed, and moved toward the bathroom. She stood in front of the mirror and pinned up her hair. She began to hum the new Adele song as she turned sideways and patted her growing stomach. "Three down, six to go," she said.

As she looked in the mirror, Mei saw a brief image of a mass of people looking upward, then a bright light. She shook her head until the image disappeared and was forgotten.

Mei showered in the steamy bathroom while singing an Etta James song. When she got out of the shower, she put her hair up in a ponytail, put on jeans with the waist snap undone, and pulled on a Colorado Rockies sweatshirt. She headed into the main part of house, then into the kitchen guided by the aroma of maple sausage and pancakes laced with vanilla flavoring.

"How'd you sleep?" David asked.

"Okay, I guess."

"That doesn't sound good. More bad dreams?"

"The usual. I guess the boys are keeping me awake."

"I read women have weird dreams when they're pregnant."

"These certainly qualify as weird," Mei said.

"What's up for today?"

"I'm going into town to do some baby clothes shopping. Wanna come?"

"I have to go to Madrid today for a meeting. I'll be back for dinner," David said.

"Get back early so we can watch *Casablanca* and have popcorn."

"Didn't we watch that last month?"

"So what? I love Ingrid Bergman in that film."

"Okay, I'll be back by seven," David said as he kissed Mei good-bye and walked out the door toward his vehicle of choice.

Later that day. downtown Aspen was virtually deserted. Mei went from store to store and quickly purchased the things on her list. Each purchase was made with gold and silver coins. After going through several stores, she finally entered her favorite— the Main Street Bakery and Cafe.

She ordered cinnamon apple hot tea and sat by the window. She nibbled on a croissant for nearly thirty minutes as she stared out onto the nearly empty street. The waitress approached and asked, "More tea, Mei?"

"Yes, thank you, guess I'm getting too predictable," Mei said with a smile.

After several more minutes had passed, a man wearing a UCLA sweatshirt entered the cafe and sat two tables away from Mei. He ordered Irish coffee and an apple Danish that had been baked only minutes before. Mei couldn't see the man looking at her. After fifteen more minutes of the man staring at her, Mei finished her tea and got up to leave. The man followed her out the door.

Mei ambled down the sidewalk, stopped at a bicycle shop. and looked in the window. The man from the bakery came up beside her. "A lot safer to ride bikes these days than before," he said.

"Guess that depends on how you ride," Mei said with a laugh.

"That's true. Hi, my name is Stephan. Visiting for a few days. What's the best place in town for dinner?"

"Lots of good places...anything on Main Street will be good. Have fun on your visit."

Mei walked away, but Stephan followed her several paces behind. After a few yards, Stephan had a question. "Mei, do you remember Robert?"

Mei stopped in her tracks; a snippet of Robert's face flashed in her brain.

"Excuse me? I know many men named Robert."

Stephan walked up to Mei. "This Robert was the former president of the United States. Kind of hard to forget him."

"I never met him."

"How about Billy? Or Abir? Father Peña? You surely must remember John."

Mei had a quizzical look on her face. Micro pictures of the men Stephan had mentioned exploded in her brain.

"I don't know these people...excuse me, I have to go," Mei walked away from Stephan.

"Remember MIT?"

Mei stopped again but didn't turn around.

"Of course. I taught there."

"Why'd you leave?"

Mei continued a slow walk with her back to Stephan. For several beats, she didn't answer. Then she turned and said, "After the asteroid, there were very few left to teach...I left MIT and then I...I came here."

"Are you aware you and I have met before?"

"I don't think so." Mei said, then turned and began to walk away from Stephan again.

Stephan walked around Mei, turned and faced her, forcing her to stop.

"I first met you at David's house here in Aspen almost four years ago. Then I saw you in Boston not long before the asteroid."

Mei stared at Stephan. A snippet of her office at MIT with Stephan, Billy, and the rest of the group raced through her brain.

"I'm sorry...I don't remember you and I have to get back home."

Mei walked around Stephan and started back down Main Street.

"Billy told me to tell you; 'it was going to miss.'"

Mei froze in her tracks. She could see snippets of the computer screen at David's Fisher Island house containing the thousand locations that were destroyed by the beams. The image lasted several seconds.

"I don't know a Billy..."

"Sure you do. Long-haired, good-looking guy. Worked at SETI. Pretty smart dude."

Billy's image flashed. "What do you want?"

Again, Stephan walked around Mei and faced her. "We need to talk, Mei."

"About what?"

"About the asteroid."

"What about it?"

"Do you believe the story of what happened?"

"Story? Everyone knows what happen. There was a malfunction during the destruction of the asteroid. The beam hit the asteroid, and there was a form of refraction that created a deadly splintering of the beam. Thousands of beams then hit the Earth and 75 percent of the world's population was lost."

"That's one hell of a malfunction."

"Had the asteroid hit Earth, everyone would have died, and the planet turned to ash," Mei said.

"If it would have hit."

"It would have hit. No question it would have hit. All the calculations confirmed it. I ran the numbers myself."

"Not everyone agrees with those calculations."

"Those people are wrong. What's your point?" Mei asked impatiently.

"My point is a question to you. What if the asteroid was going miss Earth all along? Why would the Alliance have needed to destroy the asteroid if they knew it was going to miss the Earth?"

"It was going to hit Earth." Mei said in almost robotically.

"You didn't answer my question—why would the Alliance destroy the asteroid that killed five billion people if they knew it was going to miss the Earth?

"If the asteroid had been on a path to *miss* Earth, we would have known that months in advance, but our calculations showed beyond any doubt that the asteroid was going to hit the Earth precisely where..."

"Mei, the calculations were wrong, because the data was wrong."

"The calculations were…"

"You're not listening, Mei, the data was bullshit. You still haven't answered my question. If the asteroid was going to *miss* Earth, would the Alliance have needed to destroy it?"

"There would have been no need to destroy it if...," Mei answered.

"Exactly. No need to destroy it, so why was it destroyed?"

Mei was silent for several moments, then moved to a bench in front of a florist shop, sat, and stared vacantly into the street.

"Mei, your calculations were not the only ones that were wrong. Everyone else's calculations on Earth were also wrong. Someone fed faulty data into the internet and every on-line computer in the world like a radio signal. Everyone was wrong in their calculations except someone who used a slide rule."

Mei heard Billy say "a fucking slide rule." She saw her leather slide rule holder in her hand.

"That's ridiculous. Why would anyone do such a thing?" Mei said softly.

"Maybe some folks who like the weather here on Earth," Stephan said.

"What are you talking about? Everyone knows the Alliance has been on Earth for hundreds of years."

"Maybe they thought we were fucking up the place. And there were too damn many of us and not enough of them."

"You aren't making any sense," Mei said.

"Everyone knows the Alliance can't kill the inhabitants of other planets. It's some kind of fucking intergalactic rule. But they don't stop people on Earth from killing their own. Hell, we've done that all by ourselves since the Stone Age." Stephan's voice was harsh.

"Over five billion people died because of the successful effort to destroy the asteroid. David and the Alliance did everything they could to save the planet and the people of Earth. The deaths of all those people was a tragic, unavoidable accident."

"Is that why the asteroid was destroyed seventeen seconds *before* all those people were killed?" Stephan asked.

"It was instantaneous."

"Bullshit. All those people died *after* the asteroid was vaporized."

"That's not true. The asteroid was hit, and instantaneously the beam reflected to the surface of Earth and people were accidently killed. It was a terrible accident, a malfunction. But two billion people were saved. The Earth was saved."

"The single beam that hit the asteroid did not reflect to the surface of the Earth, Mei. That's bullshit. That first beam utterly vaporized Big Ben, and it simply disappeared into thin air. The beams that hit the Earth came from another source. In fact, there were a total of three beams. The first one at 3:19:00 did destroy the asteroid as you said. The second one also at 3:19:00, was actually a series of beams, maybe a couple thousand that hit only uninhabited locations all over the world. As far as anyone can tell, not a single person died because of those beams. Not one person. Doesn't that seem a little strange to you? The third set of beams hit the Earth at 3:19:17. And they were the series of beams that killed 75 percent of the people on Earth."

"The things you're saying aren't true. Everything you said is just unfounded rumors…it was a malfunction. It was all an accident."

"Ever wonder why there was minimal physical damage to the Earth despite all those beams hitting the surface? And why vital infrastructures like roads, dams, nuclear facilities, and utilities weren't hit? Why did it seem that the biggest so-called splintered beams from the asteroid seemed to hit where the biggest crowds were? And why did the places that were hit look similar to that demonstration of the building in New York four years ago? Were all those things just coincidences?"

"You make it sound as if it was planned that way. The Alliance saved nearly two billion people."

"Mei, what do you remember about the day the asteroid was destroyed?

Mei suddenly became angry, stood up from the bench, and got in Stephan's face. "I told you before, I don't know you and have never met you or heard of those other men you spoke of. I'm tired of this conversation, and I want you to leave me alone."

When Mei brushed past Stephan, he grabbed her by the arm and handed her a card. "I told you once before you could call me anytime and I'd help…I still will."

Mei angrily pulled away from Stephan but stuffed his card in her jacket pocket as she walked away. As she did, Stephan shouted, "Mei, David lied to you. He lied to all of us. All those people…they were executed!" Mei didn't stop walking.

CHAPTER 47

BACK AT HER HOUSE, MEI held a cup of tea and stood near the sliding door that led to the deck. She stared down at a beautiful green valley. Suddenly visual images of Billy and Robert flashed in her mind. There was an image of a computer screen with flashing red dots. She saw people's faces and a red Send button.

She began to shake and dropped her cup of tea. It smashed on the stone floor. She dropped to her knees as she clutched her stomach and cried out in pain.

When Mei awoke, she saw David, a nurse, and a doctor standing over her bed. She overheard low voices in conversation. Someone said, "The fetuses are intact. It appears she suffered from low blood sugar and simply fainted."

"We'll keep an eye on her diet from now on," a second voice said.

"I want someone with her every minute," David said.

"I'll see to it."

Mei closed her eyes and went back to sleep. She dreamed of a pulsating red light.

CHAPTER 48

STEPHAN'S G-650 SAT IN A private hangar at the Aspen airport. He was at the controls preparing to head back to LA after filing his flight plan when he thought about his encounter with Mei that had taken place only an hour earlier.

He believed her when she had said she didn't remember him or any of the events leading up to or immediately following the destruction of the asteroid, or the subsequent deaths of billions of people around the world. What he didn't know was how that was possible. Had Mei been drugged? Had David somehow erased her memory like he had with the previous groups he had spoken with? He decided the answers to his questions were not in LA.

The door to the jet opened and Stephan walked down the steps carrying a garment bag. He was greeted by Carl, a mechanic. "Evening, Mr. Connor, good to see you again. I thought you were headed back to LA tonight."

"Hey, Carl. I was, but I think I'll stay another couple days. Have her ready to go Thursday afternoon, that okay?"

"No problem. Not very busy these days. Kinda lookin' for things to do."

"How's the family?"

"Fine, we're going to London in two weeks. Always wanted to see all those museums."

"How's your boy?"

"Never better. The leukemia never came back. He's healthier than a damn horse. Eats like one too."

"Good to hear."

"Need a ride back into town, Mr. Connor?"

"No, thanks, I still have my rental. Night, Carl."

"Night, Mr. Connor. See you Thursday."

Later at the Painted Pony restaurant on Main Street, Stephan sat alone in a booth in the nearly empty restaurant. He spoke with Robert on his cell.

"You see her?" Robert asked.

"Yes. Even talked to her this time."

"Anything?"

"She doesn't remember any of it. I can recall David telling us he had the ability to make all of us forget, like those groups he spoke to before us. I think he wiped at least part of her memory clean. The part around the time of the asteroid."

"What do we do now?"

"How about you calling the rest of the group and you all come out here tomorrow? Maybe if she saw all of us at once it would shake up her memory."

"I'm sure as hell not doing anything else. I'll make sure we'll all be out there by tomorrow afternoon."

"Good. How are things back in DC?"

"Getting worse here and in New York almost every day. More and more of them are coming in."

"How can you tell?"

"It's their fucking attitude. Like the rest of us are the hired help. They brought a delegation here last week suggesting that they get seats in the House and Senate so they can be fairly represented. They did the same thing in Europe and in Asia. I guess the Russians threw their asses out. But they'll be back."

"Did they make any real threats?"

"Not directly. They give the same smiles and say everything is okay and then the damn lights go out for twelve hours. You know, kind of a warning."

"How are you set for gold, Bob?"

"Okay, we'll be fine."

"Let me know if you get tight."

"Thank God you converted your stock to gold and silver before all the stuff went down," Robert said.

"Guess I was the ultimate inside trader. The gold is worth fifty times what it was then. Silver even more."

"Guess you're a pretty rich bastard. I'll call the rest of the guys and let them know you spoke with her," Robert said.

"Make sure you use this scrambled line."

"Of course. Stephan, is there really anything we can do at this point to stop them?"

"As long as they're giving the survivors everything they want, it'll be tough. There are no wars, no famine, people are healthy; medical care and housing are free, everyone has three or four cars, they can work if they want to. What's not to like?"

"The survivors and their offspring are slowly but surely morphing into a slave state. They just don't know it yet. I can see it here in the East. It's not bad now, but I can see it coming and it scares the hell out of me."

CHAPTER 49

THE NEXT EVENING, MEI AND David ate dinner as they watched *Casablanca* on cable. "Glad you're feeling better today. I was worried," David said.

"How was your trip?"

"Fine."

"I had more dreams today."

"Maybe it's all the meds."

"I dreamed of a guy I never saw before."

"Uh oh...one of those kinds of dreams? Maybe I need to work out more."

"No...it was just a jumble of things. There was the usual flash of light and the faces but this time some of the faces looked familiar, like I knew them."

David continued to focus on the genius of Humphrey Bogart on the TV screen. "I love this part."

"David, I don't remember the months leading up to or immediately following the asteroid. It's like months of my life were surgically removed from my memory."

"You know what the doctors said. That was such a traumatic time for you that your brain just shut down. I understand that happened to people all over the world. Some brains stopped processing for a while. It happened to many, many other people."

"One of the men in my dreams was named Stephan. I saw him very clearly. Even spoke with him."

David looked down at his plate of food and picked at it with his fork.

"Men in your dreams have names and you converse with them? How chic."

"He was saying crazy things."

"Well, it was a dream."

"He said the asteroid wasn't going to hit Earth. That the numbers were wrong...it was going to miss."

"You know better than that," David said.

David tried to change the subject and pointed to the TV screen. "You know, neither of them ever really says "...play it again, Sam."

"What would have happened if the asteroid had missed Earth?"

"Damn, Mei, it was going to hit Earth and kill everything and everyone on it. You know that. What's this all about?"

"I know, I know... but what if...what if it didn't hit Earth, would all those people have been killed?"

"Well, I guess not...but..."

"So the only reason everyone was killed was because of the destruction of the asteroid? I mean, that's what happened, right?"

"Yes... but...first of all, not everyone was killed. Nearly two billion people survived."

"If I recall, that's less than 25 percent of the Earth's population."

"That's about right..."

"I never heard how many of the Alliance people here on earth survived. It would make sense that it would be the same percentage, right?"

"I don't know."

"But that would make sense, wouldn't it? I mean, statistically speaking, how could there be a significant difference in the survival rate unless...unless the Alliance knew where the pieces of the asteroid were going to hit."

"I said, I don't know the numbers, but I'll find out and let you know."

"I think you maybe already know the numbers. Maybe you already know the number of Alliance deaths was zero," Mei said without emotion.

David didn't respond to Mei's assertion.

Mei got up from the dinner table and walked around the room thinking and talking. "I understand more and more members of the Alliance are coming to Earth."

"So? It's not like there isn't enough room."

"That's for sure and lots of free housing," Mei said. Mei continued to pace the room. As she did, she picked up remote and turned off the TV.

"Hey, I was watching that..."

"Know what else the guy from my dream said?"

"You mean Stephan?"

"He said, 'David lied.'"

"Did he say what I lied about?"

"Not exactly...but..."

"So let me get this straight, you are seriously questioning me about lying about something yet to be determined from four years ago, as told to you by someone from a dream, named Stephan, whom you have never met before? Is that what this is all about?"

Mei didn't answer. Instead she walked to the sliding door and went out onto the deck and saw a beautiful pollution-free sunset.

David followed Mei onto the deck and moved behind her. He put his arms around her waist and placed his chin on her shoulder. "Honey, these dreams will pass. We have a lot to look forward to with the boys coming. The business is growing. Everything is going well for us. I want you to be happy, and I know you'll be a great mother."

"I'm not crazy..."

"I know you're not."

After staring at David for several seconds, she said, "I think I'll go for a walk."

"Want some company?"

"I'd like to be alone if you don't mind."

"I understand. Don't be gone too long; it'll be dark in an hour."

CHAPTER 50

MEI TOOK THE SHORTCUT AND walked into town. Her mind reeled after what she had heard from Stephan and then David. Was one of them lying? Were they both lying? As she walked, fragments of memories entered then left her brain. She couldn't retain an image or idea. It was like a film running at ten times the normal speed, and she was unable to see anything clearly.

She walked down the middle of Main Street through the small town that appeared deserted. She pulled out the card that Stephan had given her. She stopped under a traffic light in the intersection and called the number on card. Stephan answered.

"Hello, Mei. I was hoping you'd call."

"I don't believe anything you said, but..."

"Mei, you are a brilliant woman, and all I'm asking you to do is think back to the time before and after the asteroid and tell me what you remember."

"Before, I remember teaching astrophysics at MIT. Being in Boston. Then it's a blank until I woke up and read about the destruction of the asteroid and all those people... gone."

"Almost twelve months prior to the asteroid, you were part of a seven-person group that David had assembled to help him convince the people of Earth that they had to undergo significant changes in religions, cultures, mores, and political structures, or everyone would be killed by an asteroid that only the Alliance could destroy."

"That makes no sense."

"Sure it does. David has lived here for over a hundred years. Others from the Alliance far longer. He and they knew when people from Earth heard about all the changes they needed to make, they would tell him, the Alliance, and the seven of us to go fuck ourselves. They'd rather die than change everything they knew. In essence, to change life on Earth to what the Alliance wanted, not what the people of Earth wanted."

"I'm confused. If the Alliance wanted to take over the Earth and force their will on us, they certainly have the power to do so."

"Sure they do. But first of all, they don't have the ultimate deterrent. Very simply, they aren't allowed to kill people from Earth, and they realized how hardheaded some of our folks can be. They also knew the people of Earth would fight the Alliance to the death rather than make all the changes the Alliance wanted."

"Then what was the asteroid all about?" Mei asked.

"The asteroid was real but the timing was simply by chance. That big

129

piece of rock was nothing more than a convenient tool, a prop, a rationale, to make the people on Earth make the changes that the Alliance wanted, including a massive drop in population."

"What did David have to do with all this?"

"That's where we came in. He convinced the seven of us that Earth was going to be hit, and the only way the Earth could be saved was by having the Alliance destroy the asteroid before we became toast. But there was a catch. Before the Alliance would agree to save the Earth, its citizens would have to agree to some very tough changes. Very fundamental changes that would impact everyone's life all over the planet. But those changes would also make the Earth a far better place for people from the Alliance to visit or call their new home."

As she spoke to Stephan, Mei walked down the middle of a deserted Main Street.

"What kinds of fundamental changes are you talking about?" she asked.

"All kinds; eliminate organized religions, erase all boundaries between countries, eliminate existing governmental structures, ban use of fossil fuels, but most importantly, a drastic reduction in population."

The reds dots on a computer screen flashed through Mei's head.

"Don't you see—the asteroid was a ruse. It was never going to hit Earth, and David knew that. So he provided everyone on the planet with data that was false, so all of us thought the Earth was totally fucked. It wasn't."

"But the Alliance *did* destroy the asteroid, and that's how all those people died. It was an accident."

"The asteroid was destroyed seventeen seconds *before* the people around the globe were vaporized. That rock didn't break into pieces, nor did the initial beam splinter on contact with the asteroid, so that initial beam couldn't have caused the deaths of five billion people. The asteroid's destruction was not the direct cause of all those people dying. Nor did the second beam cause those deaths since those beams hit uninhabited areas. Those five billion deaths were caused by a third beam seventeen seconds later."

"So why did those people die? Are you saying the Alliance killed them on purpose?"

"The Alliance can't kill people from other planets," Stephan said.

"So how...?"

"Only people from Earth can kill people from Earth."

As Mei walked, she had her head down and was staring at the pavement. As a result, she didn't see David in the street and proceeded to walk directly into him as he stood in middle of the two-way road.

"Oh...I didn't see you!"

"Obviously. I think you need to be more careful when walking and talking," David said.

Stephan heard the conversation and clicked off the call from his end. David took Mei's phone from her and checked "recent calls." It said, "Unknown Caller."

"What are you doing?" Mei asked as she tried to grab back her phone.

"Would it do any good to ask who you were talking to?"

"Would it do any good to ask you about a group of seven people you rounded up to help with your plan? The Alliance plan?"

"Let's go home and talk."

David grabbed Mei's arm. She twisted away.

"Leave me alone! I want to know the truth!"

"Don't be foolish..."

David reached for Mei's arm again, and as she tried to move away, she tripped and fell to the pavement. As she lay there in the northbound lane, a pickup truck driven by a teenager came speeding through and bore down on David and Mei.

David turned and saw the pickup. He ran toward it, waving his arms trying to protect Mei. The driver saw David and swerved away from Mei but in doing so slammed directly into David, knocking him thirty feet into the air. He came crashing down onto a parked car then rolled onto the street. Blood trickled from his nose and mouth. Mei screamed and ran to David. She knelt beside him. "David! David!"

His eyes fluttered open, and he whispered, "Call Dr. Winters...no one else..."

The teenager leaped from the pickup in a panic. "I never saw you guys until it was too late. Oh, God, is he dead?"

Mei calmly stood back and dialed Dr. Winters. A man she had met, although he was David's doctor, not hers. "Dr. Winters, this is Mei, David's wife. He has been hit by a car in the middle of Main Street, near the diner. He told me to call you."

"I'll be there with help in five minutes," Dr. Winters said.

CHAPTER 51

WITHIN FIFTEEN MINUTES, DR. WINTERS, with the help of two assistants, had picked up David and taken him back to his and Mei's house. They took him to the first floor bedroom, brought in what looked like two small medical bags, then told Mei to wait outside. Without saying anything to or even acknowledging Mei, Dr. Winters entered the bedroom then shut and locked the door.

Several times Mei knocked on the bedroom door and asked Dr. Winters to let her in or give her an update on David's condition. Her requests were ignored. At two in the morning, she gave up and went to bed.

The next morning, while David was still behind the closed bedroom door being treated by Dr. Winters, Mei called Stephan to let him know what had happened. "The doctor is with him now. He won't let me in or tell me what's going on. I haven't even seen David yet. I don't know why they didn't take him to a hospital."

"I have an idea why. It's vital we all get together and talk, especially now. Billy, Abir, and Robert flew into Aspen this morning, it's important that we see David before he dies. We're all in town now; we'll come to your place in a few minutes."

"Stephan, David may in fact die; he was severely injured last night, but I don't think you coming here is a good idea. Not now."

"We need some answers, and he's the only one who can provide them. We're on our way," Stephan said before he hung up the phone.

Tall, dark, athletic, and handsome, Dr. Winters looked more like an actor from a soap opera than a doctor. He sat by David's bed holding a wand-like instrument in his hand that he moved over David's body from time-to-time. When he did, readings appeared in mid-air over his bed. David's limbs were wrapped in a thin skin-colored material that gave him a somewhat mummified appearance. There was one IV tube of fluid that dispensed a light purple substance into his ankle.

"Well?" David asked somewhat impatiently.

"Well what?"

"When can I play golf again?"

"You realize you died for a few minutes last night? You also have five broken ribs, a ruptured pelvis, cracked vertebrae, a broken arm, two broken legs, a punctured lung, a fractured skull, and a big fucking bruise on your ass."

"I'm playing in a member-member in two weeks; am I in or out? Yes or no?"

"You might be a little stiff, but unless you're a pussy, you should be able to break ninety."

"Good. Maybe if you give me a note, I can still get two strokes."

"Where are you playing?"

"Melbourne."

After ten minutes of further tests and evaluations, there was a knock on the bedroom door. It was Mei. "Doctor, please, can I come in?"

Dr. Winters looked questioningly at David. David nodded.

"Sure, come on in," Dr. Winters said.

An assistant unlocked the door, and Mei entered the room. She looked shocked as she stared at David. "My God, you were so injured, I thought you were dead last night. How could you have lived through that?"

"The doc here does pretty good work, doesn't he?"

"While you guys talk, I'm going to check things out once more before I leave."

As Dr. Winters reviewed his computer and entered notes regarding David's condition, Mei tentatively approached David's bed. "You saved my life," she said.

"Loving someone can be painful at times. You know, that sounds like a 1950s song title."

"I am so confused about everything," Mei said.

"Are you and the boys okay?" David asked.

"We're fine. I stopped by my obstetrician this morning, and the boys are resting comfortably."

"That's good."

"When you're better, we need to talk. I need to understand things. Nothing is making sense," Mei said.

"We'll talk. I just don't want to lose you."

Mei reached out and took David's hand, and they spoke quietly for several minutes as Dr. Winters finished his work. "Okay, it looks like our patient has escaped the shadow of death's door for now. I'll stop back tomorrow to check him out, but he should be up in a few hours. Just take it easy tonight."

CHAPTER 52

BEFORE DR. WINTERS COULD LEAVE the bedroom, Stephan, Billy, Robert, and Abir entered. Dr. Winters sensed trouble and moved toward the group. "David, are these the guys you were talking about?"

"Yes. But let them in, Doc. it's time we clear up some things," David said.

The four men moved toward the bed where Mei sat next to David. Dr. Winters looked amused as he viewed the four men.

"We know the truth, David," Stephan said.

"Really? And what truth is that?"

"The truth about the asteroid. It was never going to hit Earth. That was a bullshit story."

"I'd say it was a perfect story except for a damn slide rule and my beautiful wife here being seventeen seconds late in pushing a little red button," David said with a smile.

Mei looked at David in shock. "You mean you lied to all of us about the asteroid? You lied to me?"

"Well, technically yeah, but there was a significant element of truth to the story. The Earth *was* going to be a dead planet in a little over a hundred years—that part was true. And since that part was true, the Alliance had decided that Earth was, in a word, history. And unlike other similar situations where we helped a planet recover when it was going in the wrong direction, we determined that you guys were so hardheaded you would never change."

"But why did you lie?" Mei asked. "Why?"

"Look, we tried to talk to people around the planet for over twenty years, you know, get them to understand what was happening to Earth, and the options that we could provide like we did with you guys. But every other group we spoke to before you said, 'No dice, we won't change.' So we said fuck it, let them kill themselves. But then I ran into Father Peña, and he convinced me to give it one more try. So we discussed the problems with him for over three years and provided him with a list of about fifty people we had selected as a possible fourth and final group. That's how you guys were selected."

"David, was the asteroid just a ruse?" Stephan asked.

"Actually, it was more of a coincidence. Or fortunate timing, depending on your point of view. We had been following Big Ben for a few hundred years and knew it was potentially dangerous. We knew it could hit Earth if it was knocked off course by a single degree if it came into contact with even a small amount of space debris. But then we got the idea that ole Big Ben could be a valuable tool and make our job easier if we played him the right way."

Mei had moved off the bed to the back of the room and sat down on a chair. She couldn't believe what she was hearing from the man she thought she loved. How could he have…?

"Look, here are the hard, cruel facts—the people of Earth were, in the end, a mistake. We messed up. We tried to build a new species, but it simply had too much dumb in it. Even giving it our DNA wasn't enough."

"So you decided to eradicate an entire civilization because you didn't like the direction it was going?" Stephan asked.

"Stephan, it wasn't going anywhere. The Earth was a dead planet walking. You guys had a spectacularly beautiful place to call home, a place a lot of other intelligent, appreciative folks would like to live, but you guys were killing it and yourselves. It was too late to stop that process. Our scientists, who are pretty good at this stuff, calculated that virtually every living thing on Earth was going to be dead by 2130."

"But wasn't that our right? After fifteen thousand years, didn't we earn the right to kill ourselves if we wanted to?" Abir asked.

"Hell no, you didn't! Like I've said, I've grown fond of this place and had an idea for a partial elimination and rebuilding process. Kind of like human redevelopment."

"Your arrogance and condescension are beyond words. You play God and…"

"I thought we covered that God thing, Abir. By the way, while we don't believe in a bunch of comic-book gods like you guys do here, with all your organized religion bullshit, we do have respect for and hold out the possibility that there is something in the universe that binds all sentient living things together. Call it a spirit of the living, a collective unconscious, or just a group of life forms that like beautiful sunsets.

In short, your God isn't big enough to cover the entire universe. That's why we're still searching, seeking answers, and even hoping that one day we will discover what links all of us. You can call it a god if you like, or anything else for that matter. The bottom line is, we realize there are still secrets out there that one day we'll learn the answers to. But you guys don't want to learn and furthermore don't care to learn. You just fall back on fairy tales and religious mumbo jumbo that is thrown out to the masses for fun and profit. That not only makes you ignorant, it makes you dangerous."

Billy pulled a pistol from his pocket and pointed it at David. "Alliance members are coming to the Earth in droves and forcing people from Earth to work for them, enslaving them."

David ignored the weapon that Billy had pointed at him.

"Enslaving them? Isn't that bit melodramatic?"

"What would you call it, asshole?"

"I would call it career equilibrium. Alliance members have always been in charge of the key technological and scientific development on Earth for hundreds of years. While you guys, the original people of Earth, have always been placed in roles consistent with your intellect, or lack thereof."

"What do you mean, in charge?" Robert asked.

"Mr. President, I hate to be the bearer of bad news, but all of you in this room have lived among the functionally illiterate and chronically ignorant of the universe for hundreds of years. Without our people in charge, such as da Vinci, Newton, Plato, Aristotle, Galileo and others, who opened up intellectual doors, your fellow Earth-folk would still be praying to the Druids and trying to learn to write."

"You mean all those guys were from the Alliance? I don't believe it," Robert said.

"There are more: Kepler, Darwin, Tesla, Hawking, and Planck. We even had our folks in the arts and music side—people like Bach, Mozart, Shakespeare, Billie Holiday, Bob Dylan, Marvin Gaye, and Barbra Streisand were all Alliance descendants."

Billy raised the pistol and placed it inches from David's face. "You really are an obnoxious prick. We all listened to your bullshit before, and now five billion people are dead. We aren't listening to any more of your lies."

Dr. Winters moved toward Billy and David. "Stay where you are, Doctor, " Billy warned.

Dr. Winters stopped then said, "Please, Billy. I'd like to go home. Don't make a mess here and make me clean it up. Besides, I can fix whatever damage you cause."

"You guys kill 75 percent of the inhabitants of Earth, and you act like it was like killing rats in a fucking barrel," Billy said.

"Rats are actually tougher to kill. They're way too smart to gather in the open to look up in the sky at bright shiny objects being blown up. Besides, we didn't kill anyone," Dr. Winters said.

"Maybe not directly but..."

"The Alliance is rather precise on that *directly* and *indirectly* distinction," Dr. Winters said.

"Jesus, you guys are cold bastards," Billy said.

Moving slowly and wincing, David got up from up from his bed and moved to the bar where he grabbed a beer, snapped it open, and took a drink. He turned and faced the group.

"Let me ask you guys something. Have you even given any thought as to why you're as successful as you are as individual humans here on Earth?"

No one from the group responded.

"Is it because you're lucky? Just worked harder than everyone else? Right place, right time bullshit?" David asked.

David walked slowly to the bedroom window in black pajamas. He stared out the window with the beer in his hand.

"Here's another question. Before the asteroid, many people killed themselves because they could not bear to live with change. After the asteroid, even more people killed themselves because they couldn't bear to live without some of their loved ones or have the life they had before. You guys seemed to cope. Why is that?"

David turned from the window and moved beside Mei, then stroked her hair.

"Finally, you come here today and if I may be so bold, you seem to be a bit half-hearted in your intent to kill someone whom you believe killed three-fourths of your fellow humans. Why is that? I mean, where is the outrage, gentlemen? The need for revenge?"

Billy let the gun fall to his side.

"Are these rhetorical questions, or are you going to bless us with the answers?" Stephan asked.

David smiled at Dr. Winters, then the group. "C'mon guys, we're on the same team here."

"What the hell are you talking about?" Billy asked.

"Do you think I picked you guys out of the fucking phone book?" David asked.

After several moments of silence, Mei looked up at David with recognition on her face. "We're them," she whispered.

"Folks, we have a winner!" David said.

"My God," Stephan said.

"You mean we're...?" Billy began a question he couldn't finish.

"Let's make this easy. None of your mommies and daddies are from Earth, which is one reason they are all still living. They came from Alliance planets two hundred years ago. In Mei's case, three hundred years ago," David explained.

"We keep track of our own," Dr. Winters said with a grin. Then he added, "The reason you guys and your ancestors were more successful is that you're much smarter than the other walking mental midgets who live on this rock. That's all. It's really simple."

"How did all those people die after the asteroid was destroyed?" Mei asked quietly.

The room was quiet. No one responded to Mei's question.

"Are you going to tell her, David, or should I?" Stephan asked.

David turned and walked toward from Mei. "Mei, anyone who was born on Earth is not considered an Alliance citizen and as a result, they can do things here that we can't do."

"What do you mean?"

"He means that even though we're like him biologically, we can kill as many people on Earth as we want. Or as many as he wants us to kill, because he can't. He's not allowed to."

"That is an interesting, albeit viable technicality," David said.

Silence fell over room again. Mei rose and walked to the window. For several moments, she stared out at the snow that had begun falling.

"It was me. That's why I can't remember," Mei said softly as if she were talking to herself.

"Mei, I told you before, your bravery and ability to act saved billions of people on Earth who would have without question died. Maybe not today, or next year, but everyone on this planet would be dead within a hundred years without you taking the action you did."

"I killed billions of..."

"Mei, everyone in this room has at least 75 percent Alliance blood in their veins. But you, like the doctor and I, have 100%. That's why you were able to do what you did. You knew what was needed. It was the only viable option. A hybrid human fails in that situation."

"What about John and José?" Billy asked.

"Their percentages were less than 50 percent. Their human side won out, or in their cases, lost out. They decided to kill themselves rather than face change or try to get their followers to change. Foolish," Dr. Winters explained with no emotion.

"David, that first day we met here in Aspen, you said you were in "development." Is that what this is all about? A fucking real estate development project for the Alliance?" Stephan asked.

"Well, to be honest, the short answer is yes. Our people will indeed relocate to Earth in large numbers because we value what you have here including lots of space now that the overcrowding problem is no longer an issue."

Then all the survivors here on Earth will be your slaves," Robert asked.

"No more than people who already perform menial tasks for you guys could be considered slaves. You know, like the people who mow your lawn, cook your food, or wash your windows at the White House, Robert. As I said before, people will rise to the level of their capability and do what they are able to do. But unlike your world, those same people will be far better cared for than you care for your own Earth-mates today," Dr. Winters said.

David added, "The difference between you and our folks is that we will respect the planet and protect it like you wouldn't and couldn't. By the way, it was only a matter of time before some of those bad guys I mentioned who like to rob and pillage planets came by and killed everything on Earth. With us in charge, that won't happen. As the Beach Boys said, 'The bad guys know us and they leave us alone.' Great group."

"But five billion people...," Abir said almost to himself.

"Look, guys, we had a tough choice to make. We could stand by and let you kill off yourselves and move the planet past the point of no return in

138

terms of fouling the oceans, poisoning the air, and destroying all your natural resources, or we could move in and try a bit of planetary redevelopment," David said.

"You killed five billion people to build a fucking resort?"

"That sounds a bit harsh, Billy. What we really did was, first of all, save Earth from Earthlings based on what you guys were doing to your own planet. Then we also saved nearly two billion of you and will create something that the vast majority of you will define as heaven. Heaven on Earth. Are those such bad things?"

Mei, Stephan, Abir, and Billy had no answer for David. Instead they sat in silence for several minutes.

"One last thing—I also kind of lied to you guys when I said you wouldn't be able to travel to other planets. If you have at least 75 percent of our DNA, which all of you do, you'll be able to adapt to the environments on many of our planet's atmospheres. Let me tell you, if you like the Grand Canyon, Niagara Falls, and shopping on Rodeo Drive, you are really going to dig the Aggan Mountains, the golf courses on Matera, the Spax Desert, and our unique water-themed malls."

"What now?" Stephan whispered.

"Everything, now. Remember John Lennon's 'Imagine'? You know, 'Imagine there's no heaven, no hell, no country, nothing to kill or die for, no religion too?' Great song. By the way, he was one of us. That's where we are folks. It's a blank slate, a new day. The air is clean, there's no poverty, plenty of food, no one is homeless, there's free cable, no sickness, and the world is at peace. Don't you get it? It was your collective dream from the very beginning. It's your heaven. We will even continue a relentless search for a god we can all love and worship. It's what you always wished for. Prayed for. Well, look outside. It's all here. The way it's supposed to be. You all made it happen. We just helped a little," David said.

Mei walked back toward David and stared at him for several moments. She placed her head on his shoulder, and he wrapped his arms around her.

"I feel the boys kicking. How about just the four of us go to Paris for dinner tonight?" I want them to get used to French food," Mei said.

"I'll drive," David said with a smile.

ABOUT THE AUTHOR

FOR MARK DONAHUE, 30 years in senior management at two Fortune 200 firms was enough. So, he quit and decided, at long last, to write. The result was five novels released in 2020 and eleven screenplays, three of which are in pre-production as feature films. "Guess I should have left commercial real estate sooner." His readers wholeheartedly agree.

Mark resides in Ohio with wife Marsha, Mika, The Wonder Dog, and boss of the house, Rocky the Cat. Much missed, and immortalized in Mark's first novel, *Last at Bat*, the late great Wheaten Terrier Carly, watches over all of them from an honored perch on a bookshelf—where else would a writer's dog be?

www.DonahueLiteraryProperties.com

D!
DONAHUE
LITERARY PROPERTIES